Crowsong for the Stricken

ALSO BY TED MORRISSEY

Works of Fiction

Weeping with an Ancient God

An Untimely Frost

Figures in Blue

Men of Winter

Works of Scholarship

Trauma Theory As a Method
for Understanding Literary Texts

The 'Beowulf' Poet and His Real Monsters

Crowsong
for the
Stricken

a novel

Ted Morrissey

Twelve Winters Press

Copyright © 2017 Ted Morrissey

This is a work of fiction. Names, characters, places, and incidents either are the product of the author's imagination or are used fictitiously. Any resemblance to actual persons, living or dead, events, or locales is entirely coincidental. All rights reserved. No part of this book may be used or reproduced in any manner whatsoever without written permission except in the case of brief quotations embodied in critical articles and reviews.

Published by Twelve Winters Press, a literary publisher.

P. O. Box 414 • Sherman, Illinois 62684-0414 • twelvewinters. com/contact

Crowsong for the Stricken was first published by Twelve Winters Press in 2017 and is also available in a digital edition.

Cover and interior page design by the author.

Cover art copyright © 2016 M. E. Tumulty. Used by permission. All rights reserved.

Author photo copyright © 2017 Ted Morrissey.

ISBN
978-1979274616

Printed in the United States of America

Acknowledgments

These are odd tales, oddly told—which makes me especially grateful to the editors of the following journals where they first appeared: *Noctua Review* ("Crowsong for the Stricken"); *Tulane Review* ("Primitive Scent"); *Constellations* ("Beside Running Waters"); *Everest* ("Erebus"); *Black Denim Lit* ("Scent of Darkness"); *ink&coda* ("The Drama of Consonants"); *Southern Humanities Review* ("Sheol"); *The Snapping Twig* ("The Ancient World"); *Blue Bonnet Review* ("Bitterness on the Tongue"); *Lavender Wolves Literary Journal* ("Planes"); *Festival Writer* ("Season of Reaping"); and *Fiction on the Web* ("The Curvatures of Hurt"). Also, "Crowsong for the Stricken" was reprinted by *Flyleaf Journal* as the recipient of the Editors' Choice Reprint Award 2015 (issue number 20, Jan. 2016). "Beside Running Waters" was reprinted in both the anthology *Literature Today* (volume 4) and at *CommuterLit.com*. "Planes" was reprinted in *ink&coda*. Further thanks to Jim O'Loughlin, host of the Final Thursday Reading Series, for arranging and participating in a group reading of "The Drama of Consonants" at the Hearst Center for the Arts; Rachel Otwell for recording and editing my reading of "Planes" for WUIS Public Radio; Pamm Collebrusco for her valuable comments and encouragement; and the Louisville Conference on Literature and Culture Since 1900, University of Louisville, for invitations to read several of these pieces. The epigraphical statements used throughout the book are not intended as verbatim, nor even complete, quotes. All were found via the Goodreads database. I beg the indulgence of the authors and their devoted readers.

It is the nature of books that their Contents must be presented in a specific order. However, these pieces are not intended to be read as they are necessarily arranged. In fact, the intention is that the effect of each will be altered depending on the sequence chosen by the reader. To that end, page numbers are offered sparingly, if not grudgingly—perhaps something like the numbered lines of a poem. You are encouraged to read the pieces in whatever order you like.

For Melissa
always

Solitude also gives birth to the perverse, the illicit, the absurd.

—Thomas Mann

Crowsong
for the
Stricken

Crowsong for the Stricken

Crowsong for the Stricken

The surest defense is eccentricity
—Joseph Brodsky

T he village constructed a special awning on their porch above the door, hung strips of heavy opaque plastic from it to form a kind of chute or anteroom, and initiated the lottery among the men to see who would use the pole each morning to deposit a paper bag of food and medicine before their door. It was a simple, time-honored procedure: A bag with handles would be used. Standing on the strickens' uneven brick walk, the designee would use the wooden pole to place the bag on their porch, pushing through the strips of heavy plastic, slide the pole from the bag's handles when the supplies were in position, then use the pole to thump once upon the door. The stricken knew to wait a full minute before opening, to give the designee time to remove himself off their property and across the street, where the curious would gather to watch the door open and see a vague figure emerge just far enough to retrieve the paper bag, then shut the door.

The onlookers could not help but measure the length of time to open the door and retrieve the bag, to listen to the force of its shutting—and to try to interpret it all for news of the stricken, as peoples of old were said to have read bird-sign or spider-webs or the haphazard arrangement of animal bones spilled from a lacquered box.

It was a traditional two-storey house, similar to perhaps three quarters of the homes in the village, except that the council had designated it a "plague house" by unanimous vote on December seventeenth and the awning and plastic were erected on the eighteenth. It was nearly spring now and snowmelt ran in the eaves. Theirs overflowed because the rooks had nested.

EACH MORNING Thomas stood in the cold and watched. He liked to imagine it was she who opened the door. Rachel was somewhat taller than her mother and nearly as tall as her father, none of whom could be mistaken in form for the grandmother or the twins. But screened by the heavy opaque plastic it was impossible to say with certainty who appeared on the porch to take in the village's offering, its "daily bread" as many liked to say.

He wanted to call out something—Rachel? How is Rachel?—but communicating was forbidden as inappropriate, as a challenge to His will. Even the telephone connection was severed. The village would know in time, who survived and who did not; there would be a great burning in their dooryard, fired by the survivors' hand; or the house itself would be fired by the village's.

Thomas had known three firings in his fifteen years, all by the village: McCluskys, Donovans, Fergussons—their names painted in gold inside the village gazebo on the square, added to the others from before his time, some names so old the paint would begin to fleck and have to be retouched. He only recalled the Fergussons' with any clarity. When five paper bags collected on the porch, on the sixth day the firing took place at sunset. A freak wind sprang up and the fire department had to work through the night to keep the flames from spreading to the Harpers' next door. It became the mission of the whole village. Thomas and Rachel were nine but stood in the empty-bucket line passing them for hours. Even then he knew where she was, that four sets of hands separated them, and he felt a baffling hurt at the knowledge that she had no awareness whatsoever of his place in line.

It was a crisp October wind and orange embers bright in the starless night fell upon the Harpers' roof like God's wrath become visible.

Thomas often reflected on another October night, when autumn carnival was underway. His mother's rhubarb pie had won third place so the family's spirits were high on the final night of the festivities. They decided to join in the masquerade reel and rummaged through the attic to piece together their costumes. His mother dressed as Seraphina in a dark blue dress, with an old pine plank belted to her back. His sister, more dramatically, went as Flora, using a concoction of karo syrup and raspberry pulp to stain her lips and chin as if blood ran from her mouth, and attaching wads of cotton to her shoes to suggest levitation in the clouds. His father donned a canine mask and took up a walking stick as dog-headed Christopher. Thomas used a tattered brown blanket as a habit and hood, and he borrowed his sister's homemade blood to stain his hands in stigmata, wanting to be Francis, whom he loved because he spoke to animals and was thought mad because of it. He and his sister and mother wore simple white masks to conceal their identities, his sister trimming hers at the nose so as not to cover her exquisitely bloody mouth and chin.

At the reel, masqueraders divided themselves by age.

Thomas watched the costumed girls and tried to figure which one was Rachel, if she was even among them. However, the lighting was subdued in the village "barn," which was in fact a large hanger from the war-days when the village had been home to an airfield; and among the masked and milling revelers he could not begin to guess if Rachel was there.

The band was about to start the first juvenile dance when a Lucy came to him in a red-flecked white gown, her face wrapped in gauze and blood flowing from her eye-sockets. Without exchanging words, as was custom, they took hands and stepped into the square marked off on the concrete floor. Lucy was slight of frame and a few inches shorter than Thomas, as Rachel would have been, but his partner moved with grace and self-assurance that he did not associate with the girl on whom he had had a crush since grade school.

They held hands as they reeled. Colored lanterns on cables cast weird-angled shadows upon the floor. Lucy's poise infected him and Thomas danced far better than he ever had before; he danced with the confidence of a practiced adult.

Throughout the evening they partnered for several reels and Thomas became convinced Lucy was not Rachel, but this bloody-eyed girl began to supplant Rachel in Thomas's imagination. He thought of holding her close, of dancing as the married couples danced, as Christopher and Seraphina danced. He began to feel that his crush on Rachel had been childish and misdirected, that he should prefer this girl, whose confident maturity had urged him toward an awakening of his own.

At the end of the evening, adolescent boys formed one line, with adolescent girls across from them in another, arranged alphabetically beginning with Ambrose and Ada.

The band provided a drumroll then the revelers all at once removed their masks. It took Lucy a moment to unwrap her gauze—Thomas's heart pounded like a snare itself in anticipation—and even fully revealed Thomas needed a few seconds in the strange lighting to recognize the mysterious girl: Rachel, whom he had abandoned and betrayed all evening with this new girl. Rachel smiled shyly toward him but he was so ashamed he turned and rushed from the barn, into the bitingly cold October night.

THE SUN HAD NOT yet fully risen when Thomas hurried from his house toward Rachel's. For two mornings the paper bag of supplies had not been taken in from their porch. The gathering of the curious had increased in number as they awaited the designee. It had snowed lightly in the night but the sun was rising in a cloudless sky and by noontime the dusting of snow would only persist in the village's west laying shadows.

The designee—Mr. Reynolds, the village's neatly trimmed and tonicked barber—arrived and carefully positioned a third bag upon the porch then knocked once on the door with the pole and retreated back across the street to stand with the curious. Thomas hugged himself in the cold, dry air and watched the plague house for a sign. It had been nearly six months since the carnival yet shame still burned leadenly in his chest and he had not been able to speak to Rachel, who had quit regarding him at all at school and who must have wondered at his sudden change.

More than thirty minutes passed with no sign of life and the curious wandered off, one by one, to work or home or school. So did Mr. Reynolds with his wooden pole. So did Thomas finally. As he walked away he heard the rooks cawing in their eaves and the crowsong sounded like accusation.

—

AT SPRING COUNCIL, his father was given the honor of playing the role of Plague in the summer Passion; the mayor brought the good news and the black costume, so that his mother would have plenty of time to alter the Plague outfit as needed and his father would be able to learn the lines by heart. They were the same every summer but it was one thing to hear them and quite another to utter the words oneself upon the stage, erected on the square near the gazebo, with the whole village looking on.

His father tried on the costume of black crepe, its sleeves tailored to resemble plumage. Thomas could tell his father was beaming with pride to be given the honor, even with his expression hidden behind the crow-faced mask with its beak of glistening black. His mother waved her hand in front of her nose and recalled that last summer's Plague was Mr. Abernathy, a heavy smoker, and when his father removed the costume she hung it in the back breezeway.

THOMAS SLEPT POORLY, his dreams dark and jagged with foreboding. He gulped down coffee with cream for his breakfast and all but ran to Rachel's. Even still, he was not the first of the curious to arrive. A half a dozen villagers were already there, the sun just washing pink the eastern horizon, and more were arriving as Thomas joined them. The light was too weak to see beyond the opaque plastic strips but the village's assumption was that the three bags remained on the porch.

As they waited for the designee adults began to reminisce about other plague houses, about the McCluskys and the Fergussons, the Johnstons and the Mesmores, about what sorts of day it was—hot and cloudy, snowy, rainy—when the fifth offering was left untaken and the council had to order a firing. They also spoke of how the eldest

O'Brien girl emerged on the afternoon of the sixth day, her sores scabbed closed and her fever broken, to start the bonfire in her dooryard, less than two hours before the council planned to set the house ablaze. The event was twenty years before Thomas's birth and he had heard the legendary tale countless times.

A great many of the curious had gathered, fifty or more, when Mr. Reynolds arrived and confirmed that the three paper bags of supplies remained. He added the fourth then joined the onlookers. A blustery spring breeze had risen with the sun and it moved the heavy strips of plastic, making it seem once or twice that Rachel or another family member had stirred them. Each time it proved a cruel hoax and Thomas's soul sank a degree deeper in a morass of despair as he stood silently with the curious, who in contrast could not fully conceal their mounting excitement in anticipation of the tragedy.

Again he was the last to leave and again the rooks taunted him.

As the day wore on he became increasingly restless and agitated. At dinner everything his family said and did added to his agitation, from the mundane reports of their days to the scraping of fork-tines against their front teeth. When he could stand it no longer, Thomas asked to be excused and went up to his room. Alone, his thoughts were no less agitating. One in particular came to him again and again imposing itself on his mind like the belief of the overzealous.

Thomas washed his face and brushed his teeth but with no intention of going to bed. In the dark Thomas kept vigil at his bedroom window listening to the house subside to quiet and watching a nearly full moon ascend above Hollis Woods. Clouds were few and thus moonlight illuminated the village streets, which was not to the advantage of Thomas's design.

However, he was supported by good fortune, perhaps as a sign from Him, and when the house was perfectly still, going on one o'clock, Thomas stole from his room fully dressed, shoes in hand, and went cautiously but directly to the breezeway. Though he was seeking it, Plague unsettled him hanging there as a black figure against the moonlit dark of the yard. He was counting on the costume's profound blackness as he pulled it on, clumsily hooking the front closures and even putting on the ebon mask.

He hoped Plague rendered him invisible.

ON THE FIFTH MORNING the curious, now more than seventy strong, were surprised to discover there were no bags on the porch of the plague house. Praise God, Blesséd Jesus, Thanks Be Almighty—even as there was an air of disappointment and onlookers dispersed more speedily. No one came out to retrieve this newest offering, yet none of the curious deemed it strange.

Nor did the rooks protest in their secure nests.

THE GNAWING in her stomach woke her. The sheets clung heavily to her damp skin. She was weak, terribly weak, but the fever was abated, and when she switched on the small lamp next to her bed she saw that the sores on her hands were scabbed over. She felt her face and discovered the same. She became aware of the profound stench in the house.

She must learn what has become of her parents and grandmother and brothers but first she must regain some strength. Her nightshirt was pocked with stains of dried blood. In the mirror appeared a ghost of a girl, a revenant of pestilence. As she made her way downstairs she had no choice but to note the silences of her family's rooms.

She had to rest a minute on the bottom stair, her head against the banister. There was little light in the house and the mantel clock within view was silent as no one had wound it in who knew how long. There was blackness in the outline space that ran along the edge of the window's drawn shade but whether it was the blackness just beyond sunset or that just before dawn she could not say.

Half dozing on the stair she wavered between a frightening dream state and a more frightening state of lucidness. How long she remained such was unclear, as was whether the noises coming from the porch were from a state of sleep or one of wakefulness. She thought of the food and medicine on her doorstep and knew that she must wait a full minute after the knock—but her flickering consciousness kept no sense of time.

The gnawing made her believe time had passed and she forced herself to a standing position. With more ease than she would have suspected she went to the door and pulled it open. Her mind must have been feverish still, for in the queer light was an enormous crow—an hallucination conjured by hearing the rooks' constant rustling in the eaves these many months.

The shock was too much and Rachel collapsed upon the door's threshold.

THOMAS, EQUALLY STARTLED, dropped the bag of supplies, spilling them across the porch, and began to bolt . . . but even before he could escape through the strips of plastic he observed Rachel fall. He stopped. He saw this waif of a girl crumpled in a heap but he also saw the door of the plague house standing agape—open portal to horror and death. In spite of the crow-faced mask the stench reached him, nearly corporeal in its potency.

He felt he loved Rachel, had issued countless prayers for her survival in the plague house, but suddenly she had transformed into the very personification of Death, of Pestilence, as if a character from a Poe story—except this was no storyteller's tableau. He feared her and pitied her, yet he also was afraid of being found here. . . .

In desperation he thought that maybe the costume's mask would offer some protection, the way a surgeon's does. Thomas hastily returned the articles to the paper bag, reached across Rachel's insensible form to deposit it inside, then gathered her in his plumed arms and stepped across the threshold.

After shutting the door, he placed her on a sofa then went through the contents of the paper bag, where he found powdered milk and farina. So he went to the kitchen, uniquely foul with odors, and ran tap water to prepare a kind of pabulum. The pipes trembled and moaned for want of use.

He sat in a chair that he had positioned next to the sofa and carefully spooned the pabulum past Rachel's cracked and bloody lips. Without fully waking she worked her swollen tongue to swallow the tasteless paste. He knew not to overdo it so after only a dozen tiny spoonfuls he put the bowl aside and let her rest. For a long while he looked through the eye-holes of Plague at Rachel's ravaged form, so thin her hands—the hands that he held during the reels while convincing himself Rachel was someone else, someone more desirable—seemed almost transparent, her cheeks were sunken and shadowed, and the black scabs stood out like leeches on her face, neck and arms.

He placed his hand on her lusterless brown hair and felt the scabs on her scalp. Tears began to burn his eyes.

He rose from the chair and started upstairs. The stench intensified with every step. He needed to know of Rachel's family. Room by room he discovered each in an agonized pose of death. Each had died alone. Her mother and father were in separate rooms, as was her grandmother, and even the twin boys were putrid and bloated within their own lonely spaces. He fought the nausea that would force him to remove his mask.

Downstairs, Rachel appeared to be merely sleeping now. There was a crocheted afghan on the back of the sofa which he used to cover her against a chill. He sat quietly for a long time just listening to her rhythmic breathing, perhaps even dozing himself. . . . She stirred and it seemed she was waking. The idea of Rachel opening her eyes to crow-faced Plague was more than he could bear so he removed the mask. He held his breath for longer than a minute but at last had to breathe normally. Before he could consider too deeply what it meant to inhale the house's corrupt air, she awoke, disoriented:

She asked, Am I dreaming?

At that moment there was a single sharp rap on the door.

Yes, he replied, starting from his seat.

He replaced the mask before gripping the brass knob.

MR. REYNOLDS WAS STILL on the brick walk when the sound of the door opening arrested everyone's attention. They watched the darkly opaque figure beyond the strips of plastic. The form paused for a moment before its plumed arms separated the plastic and it stepped into the light of day.

They say several of the curious were overcome and fell breathless to their knees, crossing themselves and mouthing prayers to the Redeemer.

They say Plague then walked the streets of the village—a murder of crows cawing in advance of his black course.

Primitive Scent

Primitive Scent

No one has imagined us
—Adrienne Rich

Lucifer lived in a cave in Hollis Woods. His head was equine in both size and shape, and he stood upright on taloned feet while his hands were hooked claws, misleadingly short of reach, it seemed, for in fact he could snatch your soul before you were even aware of its being in eternal danger. The trail leading to the cave was well known but strictly off limits.

Such was the legend that the children grew up hearing, told to them by elders who had grown up hearing it too. Francine and her father moved to the village from a northern county, and she did not know where Lucifer lived until one day when Rebecca told her. It was summer, only a few weeks after Francine and her father had moved in to the old O'Brien house, and Pastor Phillips had his daughter befriend Francine to ease her transition into the congregation, community, and eventually school, which would begin after Silvanus's Day.

Francine preferred to be called Frankie though here it struck people as undignified and even unnatural. Rebecca thought her restless to the point of being angry, but an anger that was just under the surface of an outwardly calm, disinterested demeanor. She thought Frankie's anger was like the white carp in the pond on Old Man Stevenson's farm. They swam beneath the surface milling about until the slightest thing disturbed the water—a grass blade, a skimmer bug, a crust of sandwich bread—then the fish would break the surface, their mouths greedily agape, foregoing their natural world for the unsustaining air. It seemed little would be required to call forth Frankie's anger. Rebecca assumed that what was at the heart of Frankie's anger was being transplanted here, to this backwater little village, when she was used to a more bustling kind of life.

They had been to Shirley Donaldson's for lemonade and to listen to music on the radio. If the conditions were right and if Shirley's antenna was just so, she could pick up the city station and hear the newest releases. Shirley's parents did not wholly approve of her listening to the station, with some of its unwholesome and unchristian song lyrics, so the heavily freckled redhead was indulging in a bit of riskiness for her guest's sake to tune the radio to the city station. Frankie made only a halfhearted attempt to mask her boredom, so after an hour Rebecca claimed to have some chores undone at home, and she and Frankie left the Donaldsons'.

They were walking along the village square, totally abandoned at this time on a summer afternoon, and Rebecca suddenly ran into the gazebo on the square and sat in the shade. After a second or two Frankie reluctantly followed. There was room on Rebecca's bench, which ran the length of one of the hexagon's sides, so Frankie sat there too.

The girls were both fifteen, with bodies that were only just beginning to hint at the women they would become. They sat quietly, knowing that each was listening to a wasp that bounced along the rafters, apparently unable to find its way out in spite of the structure's openness.

Shirley's nice, Rebecca said, picking at the hem of her shorts. It was nice of her to have us over.

Opting to neither agree nor disagree, Frankie turned her attention fully to the wasp. Upturned, Rebecca noticed for the first time the green of Frankie's eyes—green like the underside of the leaves of red maples, the side that only reveals itself during a summer storm. She thought that they complemented her dark skin and hair—hair that Frankie merely swept to one side, allowing it to continually fall across her face, with her right eye constantly obscured. Just as it was now, and Rebecca was irritated to the point of wanting to sweep it into place and tell Frankie to get a barrette or a headband, something.

She understood, at least vaguely, what bothered her was that Frankie allowed herself the freedom to wear her hair however it fell, and that her clothes, like this blue-striped skirt and white cotton blouse, were worn as loosely and carelessly as if she had had to borrow them from someone in a pinch. While Rebecca put so much effort into taming her blond curls, and matching her headband to her blouse, and ironing a sharp crease in her shorts and skirts. Yet no one seemed to notice or care—she rarely received a compliment, and Rebecca could not help but notice how the boys in the village looked at Frankie, some of the married men too, even Rebecca's father.

It all caused Rebecca to feel a restless sort of anger of her own and she wanted to show Frankie that she possessed something that Frankie did not—and the knowledge of Lucifer's den burst forth:

There's a cave in the woods where Lucifer lives—right over there, and she fanned her arm toward Hollis Woods, somewhere beyond the post office and Mr. Reynolds's barbershop.

Frankie continued watching the wasp. Lucifer? The devil? She finally looked at Rebecca. Sweat had gathered on Frankie's upper lip. Right over there, in Haley Woods?

Hollis Woods, yes.

How can that be?

The form of the question took Rebecca by surprise. How? She was prepared to argue Lucifer's existence in the cave, not *how* it was possible.

Frankie did not bother waiting for a reply. Have you seen him? Lucifer?

No—but he's there, we've known for a long, long time; people here have known forever.

So we could go to this cave right now, this very minute, and see him?

He's Lucifer—we don't *want* to go there—besides, the trail is off limits.

Frankie began laughing—laughing out loud like boys laugh among themselves at a joke no one should tell, and Rebecca wanted to slap the laugh from Frankie's merry face, the dark hair falling in front of it.

It's true, she said meekly.

Frankie stopped laughing to ask, So you just accept that the devil's there, in the cave? Without having seen him yourself?

Rebecca had nothing to say.

Tomorrow I'll meet you at your house, let's say nine o'clock, and we'll go check out this cave of yours.

Rebecca began to protest but Frankie bounded down the steps of the gazebo and headed in the direction of her house. For the first time since moving to the village she seemed happy. Rebecca watched the sunlight glint off Frankie's hair, her suntanned legs bouncing along the concrete walk.

The black wasp ceased its futile sorties against the rafters of the ceiling and flew out of the gazebo to disappear on the hot summer air.

That night Rebecca tried eating her mother's casserole but every bite made her ill so she excused herself to her room. While her family went about its nightly business—it was Thursday so her father was beginning to write his sermon in earnest—Rebecca tried to distract herself from thinking about Frankie and her determination to visit Lucifer's cave, but nothing worked and her nausea grew worse and worse. She wished that she had never mentioned the cave to Frankie, she wished that Frankie had never moved to the village. What was she doing here anyway? She and her father clearly did not fit in. Her father sold seed and he could do that living anywhere along his route—there were plenty of larger towns that would have suited him and Frankie.

Rebecca reached over and pulled the waste basket closer to her bed; she was certain she was going to be sick. The radio was playing a familiar song but the song itself seemed to be making her nausea more acute. She picked up the radio from her desk to shut it off. Instead her fingers found the tuner knob and began working it toward the city station. When she thought she might be close she adjusted the volume so low that she could barely here the crackling static. Her heart raced and she glanced at her closed door—she wished that she had a lock on it, like her parents' door.

There . . . the city-station music came from the radio's speaker, half music and still half static. She twisted the antenna . . . there, better. Rebecca listened with the radio against her ear. It was a love song, one that she had never heard.

The music calmed her and later she fell asleep with the

radio next to her pillow, the risqué music trickling gently into her ear. She felt a touch of shame but the music was comforting nonetheless.

In the night she dreamed of the fish in Old Man Stevenson's pond. She was floating in a tractor tire, her legs draped over the edge so that only her feet were in the water, and her posterior, through the center of the tire. She was enjoying the coolness of the pond water, watching a wasp-shaped cloud in the otherwise pure blue sky. But with the first nibble on her toe she remembered the carp, flesh-white and as long as her shinbone. She tried to lift herself out of the water, the tire bobbling as if it may tip over altogether. She saw the fish's sucking mouths and their black eyes, glassy and vacuous. The cloud moved before the sun, plunging Rebecca into a night-like darkness on the pond, thousands of fish swarming upon her. . . . She awoke tangled in twisted bed sheets. The radio, with its dead batteries, had fallen to the floor.

At nine o'clock Rebecca was sitting on her front porch drinking a glass of juice. It was cool in the shade of the porch but it promised to be a beastly hot day, the first of the summer. Her illness had returned and she could barely swallow the sips of juice.

Perfectly on time, she saw Frankie coming up her street—a bulky cotton bag on her shoulder. She stopped at Rebecca's front steps.

What's all that? said Rebecca, nodding toward the bag.

Flashlights, bug spray, apples in case we get hungry.

Rebecca had planned to bring nothing, perhaps because she did not believe they would really go to the cave. Yet she knew Frankie would not change her mind—for one thing, she was determined to prove Rebecca wrong . . . to prove the whole village wrong.

The screendoor opened, startling Rebecca, and her father stepped onto the porch. Good morning, ladies—what are you up to so early this morning? Pastor Philips was in beige pants and a maroon sports shirt, looking strange to Frankie not in his ministerial black. Perspiration glistened on his bald head.

Thought we might go for a hike, said Frankie.

A hike? I didn't know you'd turned my daughter into a nature lover—job well done, Miss Francine, and he winked at Frankie. Well, I'm off to the church—Mrs. Overton claims one of the organ pedals is getting mushy, and we can't have music with mushy notes in God's house. Have a good hike, ladies. Then Pastor Phillips went down the steps and turned to his pickup truck in the driveway. In a moment he was pulling away, with a honk and a last wave.

Are you ready? asked Frankie.

Rebecca knew it was futile to protest. She could simply refuse to go with Frankie but something prevented her from doing that too. It might have been pride—not wanting to forfeit the village's integrity, or simply not wanting to be wrong. As she left the comfort of her porch and began walking with Frankie toward Hollis Woods, the outskirts of which intersected with the boundaries of the village, Rebecca felt curious more than anything. She wanted to know if the legend was true. There was fear also but it did not seem precisely the fear of encountering the devil himself—though that would have made sense to her—rather it was fear complexly bound with shame, with guilt. . . .

Walking along in the rising heat and humidity, not speaking, Rebecca could not sort out all that she was feeling, nor even begin to articulate it if she tried. Meanwhile images from her dream about the white carp kept returning to her; and as unsettling as they were, she preferred them to dwelling on the task before her.

She glanced secretly at Frankie, who was a few inches

taller, and her expression was as placid and as featureless as the cloudless blue sky above them.

Rebecca had to lead the way once they reached the woods, which were noisy with insect sounds and birdsong. There was no purpose in delay so she took the winding paths that led directly to the off-limits trail. A wooden barricade was erected, white paint peeling from its posts and cross boards, and a sign with faded letters that warned NO ADMITTANCE. From what they could see the trail was overgrown but recognizable among the trees and leafy forest growth.

Frankie rearranged the bag on her shoulder and climbed over the barricade, which was only waist high and more ornamental than functional. Rebecca followed in a few seconds. It occurred to her that given what lay at the other end of the trail, the barricade might have been more substantial. Until this moment however it had always been substantial enough.

Penetrating deeper into the woods the air became cooler and heavier, the insect sounds more distinct and stranger, as if new to Rebecca's ears. In fact the woods felt altogether alien, though she had been in them to walk or picnic or play a hundred times. This part of the forest was utterly different. A strangeness came over Rebecca but it was more than the woods feeling foreign—she herself seemed changed.

The trail wound back and forth, then without warning they were standing in front of the mouth of the cave. It seemed carved into a lushly overgrown hill, and the small black entrance was situated in a way that suggested one would be walking steeply downward upon entering.

Well, said Frankie, shall we, as she fished the flashlights from her bag. She gave Rebecca one with a red plastic casing while she took a larger metal flashlight. The girls switched them on and cautiously entered the cave, Frankie leading and having to duck a little. She looked totally at ease but perhaps her heart was racing as much as Rebecca's for she reached back and took her friend's hand.

Immediately a mineral scent reached Rebecca, and a welcome coolness. Except for their scuffing shoes the cave was perfectly quiet. Shining their lights along the walls and ceiling and floor, they could see the cave was simply an empty space—there were no bats or dark-dwelling insects. Its emptiness was a relief to Rebecca. The cave was so small their lights reached its farthest corners.

You see, said Frankie in a whisper, there's nothing here. Yet she still held Rebecca's hand.

Rebecca continued to shine her light along the cave walls, the fear slowly leaving her. What's that? Her light had illuminated an odd feature of the far wall. They approached it while using their flashlights to expose the form in the rock more fully. It was the shape of some creature fossilized in the wall but mostly exposed to view. It had a horselike head except with sharp teeth in its jaw. Its spine and ribs appeared in the girls' moving lights, as did its strangely short arms, stranger still in contrast to its large legs bones. In life it must have been a fearsome thing.

It's a dinosaur of some sort, said Frankie—there's your Lucifer.

The girls continued looking at the prehistoric animal, seeing it one small piece at a time. Neither girl was inclined to release their clasping hands. In a way that did not require words they knew this would be their secret. They alone would smell the cave's primitive scent.

Beside Running Waters

Beside Running Waters

There is a sacredness in tears
—Washington Irving

They stood in line at the filling station, the candy bar and cold bottle of soda in one hand and the exact amount of money in the other, $1.17, waiting on the customers ahead of her, Mrs. Willis and her son Charles, who everyone knew was slow. Mrs. Willis, in librarian-style tortoiseshell glasses, was resolute that Charles should pay for his hot dog, soda and baseball cards by counting out the amount from his mason jar of coins— but the boy, nine or ten, kept getting confused, and he was turning crimson under his stubble of white-blond hair as more and more customers gathered behind him and his mother, who was determined not to notice the lengthening line, now stretched as far as the Eskimo Pie freezer.

She could feel the cold leaving her bottle of soda—and she wished that she'd left it in the cooler until after she'd paid—but she wasn't irritated with Charles and Mrs. Willis. The girl marveled at Mrs. Willis's love for Charles and her endurance in pursuit of his success. Though the boy would've gladly given up any of the items, perhaps all of them, to end the spectacle and retreat to the things he knew, maybe fishing, greasing bicycle chains, mimicking birds.

Those in line behind the girl didn't seem as patient; she sensed their mounting anxiety, which in turn made her anxious: Before long, she knew, the onlookers would notice her and instantly Charles's counting and recounting couldn't keep their attention.

The clink and scrape of the coins against the filling-station counter were a nuisance as she strained to hear the phrase she despised. For fifteen years she'd had a name and in a moment no one seemed to recall it. For more than eighteen months now she'd been *the dead boy's girl.*

She looked out the filling-station window, a slick of diesel on the cracked concrete glimmered rainbow in the summer heat.

Even in grade school they'd played at being boyfriend and girlfriend, and didn't mind their classmates' teasing, so the joke soon grew old and ceased altogether. Their teacher must've thought little of it when during quiet time they would unroll their mats next to each other and hold hands as naturally as cloudbreak while music or a story played from a cassette. Perhaps Miss Hollis thought the phase would pass and boy and girl would return to their predetermined state of antagonism like cat and dog—until she and the other teachers stopped thinking of it at all.

By the time they were in junior high it had long been conceded they would be together forever. She sometimes felt sorry for her friends who were in such constant turmoil over which boy liked them, or that none did, that they liked some boy who didn't know they were on the planet, while the boy they couldn't stand mooned over them day and night . . . it must've been wearisome, and she had never experienced it.

Outside a pair of boys uniformed in sleeveless shirts,

threadbare jeans and seed-company caps were filling gas cans preparing for a day of mowing. Their arms and necks, as brown as sycamore bark, were already becoming corded like their fathers'. The one in the blue cap was Everett Bishop who everyone called "Egg" except his mother; the other, in a green cap, was Dale Stupig . . . Dale and Henry had been friends, sometimes played baseball in the Stupigs' grass field when a break in chores allowed, half-empty seed bags for bases. She played a few times but could barely hit the ball, which Henry tossed toward her in a gentle arc. She stopped playing and Henry must've too.

Still too young for a license but old enough to drive the old F-150, which left behind flakes of rust wherever it had sat for more than a few minutes, Henry took them down Stevenson Lane across a finger of the Hewitts' property to a wooded stretch of Peach Creek, where spiny bluegill and pugfaced pumpkinseeds were plentiful and hungry for cricket bait in the shadowed water. Their catches would flop about in a metal bucket cooling in the Peach's terracotta mud.

One afternoon she watched the tendons of Henry's neck as he worked the hook from a pumpkinseed's throat, and her eyes followed those tendons, like metal cables, down his back, where the muscles moved beneath the sweat-damp shirt, and she took in the rounded seat of Henry's jeans, where only threads and a darker patch of blue remained as evidence of the right pocket. A feeling came over her that she knew only by reputation. Not quite sure what she was doing, she told Henry the heat was getting to her and she was going to rest in the truck.

He looked back at her strangely—the heat never bothered her. She knew in a few minutes he would join her so that she could rest her head against his shoulder, which she would kiss and taste its salt.

After that day they began fishing every chance they got. In the fall they developed a great fondness for hiking and autumnal foliage. When cold weather came, they visited friends, and the search for the perfect stand of Christmas trees became an ongoing odyssey which commenced with the first hard frost of November.

The boys were finished filling the gas cans and were coming inside to pay and probably to get something cold to drink. She shifted her weight from left to right foot and back again. Egg Bishop had been very sweet at the funeral and the days that followed, and she needed the support: she felt as empty as the Peach in winter, her will to get through each impossible day a faint trickle which at times disappeared altogether beneath a spread of ice.

Then Egg began to act like he was interested in taking up where Henry had left off, which frightened her so—to think that someone might take Henry's place—that she stopped seeing and talking to Egg. In fact, she shut herself away from every boy in town, then from everyone in town. She felt like the wine merchant in that Poe story, the one who is bricked inside the cellar wall, except she was both victim and bricklayer.

She heard mumbles of voices from behind. She couldn't look because she knew Egg and Dale were at the end of the line, which she imagined stretched around the Eskimo Pie freezer and snaked into the bread and cereal aisle. Soon it could form a U in the filling station, with the last customer standing back-to-counter next to scarlet-faced Charles Willis and his mason jar.

She thought she heard the words, and the patience suddenly drained from her like coolant from a cracked radiator. She reached past Mrs. Willis and deposited the money on the counter, more forcefully than she intended, and she rushed from the filling station. Before the door swung shut she heard a coin fall to the floor but didn't know if it was one of hers or if she startled Charles and he'd fumbled a quarter off the edge of the counter.

The day's heat fell upon her suffocatingly. She rubbered in behind the steering wheel of her Gremlin, her bare legs sticking to the black vinyl seat, which was cracked and losing padding. She had a bottle-opener on her key ring and used it. The soda was barely cool and tasted too sweet. She no longer wanted the candy bar that was melting in its wrapper on the passenger seat.

She watched the filling-station door open and Mrs. Willis and Charles came out into the sunlight. The boy had his items but he too seemed to have lost his appetite.

Unable to control it, she began retching, pushed open the car door and vomited the soda along with her breakfast of eggs and toast from three hours earlier. She wiped her chin with the back of her hand, shut the noisy door, and started the engine. Mrs. Willis, parked near the pumps, was stopped with her hand on her station wagon's door. She'd seen the spectacle of the girl being sick. It was a hard look behind the tortoiseshell glasses, a face the girl could only interpret as anger without a trace of sympathy.

She put the Gremlin in first and drove off the filling-station lot. Without considering her course she left the main street and was quickly on County Road 12. She turned on the radio to the only station it picked up clearly, the AM Christian station from a neighboring town, and recognized Porter Wagoner's "He Took Your Place" . . . *Someday he's coming back to claim his own. . . .* She felt a warm drop on her bare right thigh and thought she'd missed something on her chin but discovered she was crying: another tear fell on her left thigh.

She recognized the early symptoms of a migraine, the headache as spiny as bluegill beginning behind her eyes, the nausea, the sensitivity to light, sound and touch. She turned onto Stevenson Lane, headed for the Hewitts' property, and switched off Porter Wagoner.

Pulling away from the lane, she immediately saw the path that had formed in the grass field, worn first by Henry's truck then by her Gremlin, whose tires fit easily inside the track of Henry's F-150. The Gremlin's low-setting chassis bumped along a minute a more until she parked in the shade—heavenly shade—with the Peach running before her in both sun and shadow.

She turned off the engine and let back the seat, hoping a few minutes' rest would ease her head and stomach. Peach Creek's gentle bubbling filled her ears. She began drifting away as if carried by the Peach's steady current.

In a moment she felt the hand on her thigh, felt the fingertips kneading her damp flesh. She spread her legs to ease the hand's working, and fingers wriggled beneath the hem of her shorts. She must've emitted a little sound but all she heard was the Peach's cool waters. The hand toyed with her until she squirmed in her seat, gripping the bottom of the steering wheel as if the gunnel of a storm-tossed ship. Her lips formed sounds more ancient than words. Then the hand spread across her womb, and it was as warm and comforting as a griddlc cake, even with the calluses. It lingered there gently pressing against her flesh, and she felt the pulse against the palm as its rhythm matched her own labored breathing. She reached down and put her hands over the hand that held her womb, and rather than muffle the beating pulse, it seemed to amplify it; and the reverberations spread to her arms and shoulders and throughout her young body . . . until they returned to their genesis.

She stayed that way a long while, thinking of this miracle that must be Henry's doing. Her mind flipped through images of her future, like photos in an album. The images were blurry, though, as if the speed of the film were out of synch . . . *would be* out of synch. There would be a child, but boy or girl? The pictures were too out of focus to say. Henry's blue eyes, she wondered, her brown hair, his broadness through the shoulders, her long legs?

The hand remained on her womb, the pulse continuing to vibrate throughout her being—then she felt the kisses on her shoulder, her neck . . . she felt the peach-fuzz tickle of Henry's never-shaved lip. The kiss was upon her cheek, the lips brushing her earlobe. She heard the whisper of her name. She held tighter the hand. . . .

Miranda, but it came from another place. . . .

You all right?

She blinked at the sun-crests on the creek. Egg Bishop was at her driver-side window; someone was behind him at some distance, must be Dale Stupig. She released her seat upright, and looked at Egg, saying nothing while she started the engine and found reverse on the steering column.

In a moment, the Gremlin was speeding over the worn path. She glanced in the rearview mirror and in its jumpy image she thought she counted three figures standing watching her departure.

Tears hot as August fell upon her legs. She tried to clear her eyes before pulling onto Stevenson Lane but she was careful not to wipe the cheek where a touch of lips lingered like a final kiss goodbye.

Erebus

Erebus

One must turn away from the world at times

—Albert Camus

Besides her name, Mary Patterson was an obvious choice for the role of Mary in the Nativity play. She was an able speaker—runner-up in the county forensics tournament in extemporaneous the previous spring and third place in occasional—and she looked the part of a chaste girl, a girl unknown to men. Long brown hair, always parted crisply in the center; eyes as green as 7-UP bottles; just as many freckles across her nose and cheekbones as you'd want to try to remove with a saliva-moistened tissue, if you didn't love them so. And Mary Patterson's long-limbed willowiness would transform into a kind of grandeur in the Virgin Mother's costume of celestial blue.

Mary Patterson was ideal, and when Mrs. Hulbertson, the choir director, announced the parts at Wednesday night youth group, Mary's 7-UP eyes filled with tears and she rushed from the church basement without a word to anyone.

Outside, the season's first heavy snow lay atop the churchyard, its new crust glittering like ground mirror-glass in the moonlight. Mary had stopped on the precisely shoveled sidewalk just beyond the Methodist Church's side-door steps. Wearing only a wool sweater and denim jeans, she hugged herself against the cold, which stung the tears in her eyes and made them spill onto her freckled cheekbones.

The idea had come to her, there in the basement, when her role was announced. It was possible but only barely conceivable.

Mary's winter coat was on a peg in the church basement; her home was to the right, on Maple Street, a short distance even in the cold. She turned to her left on the brick walk.

She soon passed the square, with its gazebo capped in snow which reflected the bluish lunar light, almost like the blue edge of the jukebox in Mr. Owens's café. Mary was on Main Street. She paused a moment to capture her own phantom's gaze in the window of Mr. Reynolds's barbershop—where she went until she was old enough to visit Mrs. Abernathy's salon in the basement of her home on Willow Street—age twelve like the other girls in the village. The dyeing and curling and straightening solutions, even in their potency, only partially masked the combination of cigarette smoke and model-glue smell left by Mr. Abernathy, who used the basement whcn his wife didn't have clients.

Mary felt as thin and transparent as the phantom girl staring back from Mr. Reynolds's window. That girl was surrounded by darkness, and Mary felt that too. That, and the cold. She hugged herself again and continued walking.

Main Street intersected with Highway 12 at the village limit. The intersection was still a quarter mile ahead but already the space felt desolate, the houses less common and set back farther and farther from the street. It was as if the village was withdrawing from her, as if her life there was withdrawing, her childhood.

The sidewalk had terminated beyond the public library so Mary was treading on the side of the street, plowed snow, knee-high, embanking along the edge, when she heard the pickup truck approach her from behind, its old engine still cold and laboring. The truck rolled to a stop beside her but she kept walking, the soles of her shoes crunching the gravel and ice crystals that were now more prevalent in the street.

Anticipating her headstrongness, the pickup driver pulled forward several yards before halting and leaning across the cab's seat to roll down the passenger window.

Mary, in spite of her agitation and the darkness, recognized the truck and was not surprised to hear Egg Bishop's voice:

What are you doing, Mary? You'll freeze, get in here and I'll take you home.

She hadn't even slowed, which forced Egg to ease up the clutch and brake, in order to roll beside her. The engine threatened to cease altogether barely in first gear. Mary had stopped crying but something about the familiarity of Egg's voice (they'd known each other since first grade) and his mentioning home began the tears anew.

It blurred her vision of the road ahead.

I don't want to go home. . . . She choked on the tears.

Fine—I'll take you wherever. Or we can just drive around, whatever you want, Mary-Mary—but just get in.

Egg's using her nickname, the one she'd had since grade school, softened her mood, and she opened the pickup's noisy door and climbed onto the seat, which was still stiff and cold as the truck's heater was just beginning to blow warm.

Egg took her hand but only to feel exactly how icy it was. He released it to reach behind the seat. Here—you'll catch pneumonia. Then he helped her into the heavy canvas jacket, fleece-lined, that he used for morning chores. All the boys kept such jackets behind the seats of their trucks.

Mary struggled for a moment with the zipper but it freed itself and she was glad to have the jacket, even though at first it only made her colder. It smelled like spring lambs and winter wheat, with a sweet touch of diesel fumes.

Egg had started to move forward but it was obvious he didn't know their destination.

Take the highway, north.

It was the last thing either of them said for several miles. Meanwhile the truck's engine had warmed and it now purred contentedly as they rolled along the empty black road that rolled before them like a mourning ribbon between the silken fields of white.

They were within three miles of the Harristown blacktop, a good turn to take to begin their way back to the village.

So, said Egg, his features slightly aglow in the dashboard lights, how are you doing, Mary?

She maintained her silence while she considered Egg's features as they appeared in the queer light, which made him older, revealed the beginning lines of farmer's squint, and his teeth, with their subtle and attractive underbite, had lost their youthful whiteness: Egg Bishop was a young man who would one day be an old man in the village, perhaps sitting on the village council as his father had, or even serving as mayor like his grandfather. Possibly shedding the name Egg, to be Everett, as only his mother called him now.

Don't take the blacktop. Please.

You know where we'll be if we just keep going. There's school tomorrow.

Mary was silent as they passed the Harristown turn; then she dozed for a few moments, so that the sound of the wipers startled her.

It's snowing. Just a little.

The specks of white appeared and disappeared in the truck's low-beams. Half dreaming, Mary saw them as shattered pieces of her past mixing with bits of her future, colliding, missing, forming something new. In Mrs. Wilson's class she learned about the Greeks and their story of Chaos and Night, and fragments of the tale came to her, like the dark silence of Erebus.

What was your part? In the play—what is your part?

Egg laughed. You know I can't act my way out of a wet paper bag. I'm just a shepherd.

Shepherd is important.

Maybe, in real life. But not in the play.

Mary laughed. You'll be terrific.

A mile or more passed beneath the truck's tires.

What about you, Mary? Will you be terrific? In the play?

Mary considered the silence of Erebus then switched on the truck's radio. Already the familiar station was crackling out of range. She recognized Red Foley's fading voice: *trumpet sounds within my soul, I ain't got long . . . I'm gonna steal away home. . . .* She turned the tuner knob until the city's popular station was clear, signaled by the phrase *great balls of fire. . . .*

Pastor Phillips wouldn't approve, or Mrs. Hulbertson . . .

Or anyone. Mary increased the volume. But none of them are here.

After a moment Egg reached over and turned down the volume. I need to concentrate on the road.

Ahead, the lights of the city were caught in the gauzy snowclouds, though it was still at least thirty miles distant. They would be arriving at a bad time, hours and hours too early. But places in the city were awake all night. They would just have to wait in these sorts of places.

She glanced at Egg's aging profile and wondered if he would wait with her once he knew. So far he'd been a hero, taking her without demanding her intentions, intentions she barely acknowledged to herself.

Egg . . .

He returned her glance for a second.

Thank you, for driving me . . . and for the coat.

I don't know what we're doing, Mary. Would you want to tell me?

. . . *I'll be the vision of your happiness* . . .

I will, I will . . . but I need to rest a minute. She was suddenly exhausted, and she needed to gain control over the nausea she'd begun to feel. Churning rock salt pushing against her heart.

SNOW WAS FALLING harder in the city, clinging to the sidewalks, where piles of it had been shoved into corners. Off of Harris Street, one of the main arteries, they found an all-night diner, Don's, so they'd stopped to use the bathroom and perhaps get something to eat.

Egg sat in a corner booth. He could see the entire diner, including the front door and long, chrome-trimmed counter, along which a half dozen customers were seated eating or just drinking coffee, and behind which leaned a heavyset man of about fifty. More than a day's gray stubble stood out on his fleshy cheeks and chin, and he wore a dingy white apron over everyday clothes. Egg suspected it was Don himself.

Choosing the seat was easy: Egg had watched enough television Westerns to know the gunslinger always sat so that he could see the whole room, to avoid being taken down by surprise.

Though Don wasn't frying anything at the moment, the smell of grease, especially bacon grease, was heavy in the air, along with the strong coffee and cigarette smoke.

Mary was returned from the bathroom and she sat opposite Egg in the booth.

You want something?

I not only left my coat at church but my purse too.

That's okay, I have some money.

Mary looked at Don, who seemed enthralled by the snow falling just beyond his diner's window. Do you think they have hot chocolate?

I can see.

If not, coffee, with plenty of room for cream and sugar.

Egg went to the counter and stood next to an empty stool, which was worn red leather and dull chrome, and anchored to the dirty linoleum. Egg realized the men were mostly quiet because they were concentrating on the radio. It was on the shelf above the grill, between an open bag of C&H and a Folgers can from which protruded assorted cooking implements. They were listening to a prizefight.

. . . *jab, jab, jab, then the champ throws the right . . .*

At that moment one of the fighters, Hurricane, managed a flurry of punches, and Don waited until he heard that the barrage was over before turning his attention to Egg, who asked for two cups of coffee and two orders of toast. He returned to the booth with the cups of coffee.

It doesn't look like a hot chocolate sort of place. He placed the cups on the table then retrieved the small metal pitcher of cream from the counter.

. . . *Patterson takes another body blow but works his way out of the corner . . .*

Mary was pouring and stirring the sugar. She added cream until the coffee turned the brown of Rhode Island eggs and nearly reached the cup's lip.

They pretended to be interested in the fight but soon the bell concluded the third round, and the men at the counter broke into conversation. Don brought their toast, a pad of melting butter sandwiched between each warm slice, cut diagonally; and a basket with three jars of jelly: grape, strawberry and apple.

No words were exchanged.

Mary chose the apple jelly, while Egg spooned grape onto one of his slices, then strawberry on the other. The jellies created colorful swirling shapes spread over the melted butter, and Egg was reminded of one of the film-strip frames Mrs. Wilson showed them when they read about the Greeks and their creation story.

They enjoyed their repast while the fight filled the air as thickly as the competing scents. Egg thought about ways to bring up their purpose here—while Hurricane Jackson weathered body blow after body blow from the champ, and the snowstorm pounded the city streets, freshening the scene beyond Don's large window, the neon script of *Don's* glowing against the glass to create a halo of pink.

You must've been hungry, said Egg.

Mary was fingertipping the crumbs on her plate and touching them to her tongue. It tasted good, and not much else has. She took a drink of coffee.

The men at the counter suddenly yelped and groaned at some happening in the prizefight—Hurricane was knocked down.

There was another eruption in the diner, and Egg thought for a second something new had been reported by the radio; but it was a couple, a Negro couple had entered the diner, with urgency it seemed. Their ages were hard to determine, perhaps they were teenagers, close to Egg and Mary's grade, or maybe much older. Snow salted the boy's wool cap and the shoulders of his corduroy coat, and it lay heavily on the girl's springy hair and on the Navajo-pattern blanket draped around her shoulders. Both Negroes wore expressions of distress, and Egg noticed that the girl was heavily pregnant.

Don had returned to his place behind the counter, and for a moment he and the boy stared at each other, dumb with surprise.

We need to find the hospital, we got turned around in the storm.

The men at the counter had twisted on their stools to look at the newly arrived.

The girl's face contorted in pain and she crumpled against the boy to keep from falling. The blanket fell from her shoulders revealing a plain rust-colored dress. Egg saw that she was standing in a puddle of snowmelt and other fluids.

One of the men at the counter got up from his stool. You're not going to wait till the hospital. The man was gray with a beard that may have been a beard or merely several days' unshaven growth. He wore a dark overcoat and peered over the heavy steel frames of his glasses.

What're you saying, Doc?

The prizefight crowd on the radio broke into cheers and Don reached up and lowered the volume.

I'm saying this baby's going to arrive any minute. He was taking the Negro girl toward a booth. You there, he said to Egg, help me with this.

Egg jumped to his feet, and he and the man lifted and moved a table toward the center of the diner, leaving two worn leather benchseats facing each other. On each seat there were two ovals where the black leather had been rubbed gray over time.

Doc had the girl lie flat on the seat. She was small but still her legs extended beyond the edge of the seat, and her shoes dripped onto the floor. The Negro boy had picked up the Navajo blanket, and Doc took it from him and rolled it into a pillow for the girl.

How long since you delivered a baby, Doc?

Residency.

Beautiful.

Mary had gotten up from the booth and she was standing next to Egg, who was still next to the displaced table.

The girl was crying and in pain but doing all she could to fend off pure hysteria.

Mary knelt by the girl and took her hand, which was icy, especially her fingers. Mary was surprised: She didn't think Negroes could be cold. It's going to be all right. What's your name?

Ju—Julie.

It's going to be all right, Julie. I'm Mary.

Nice to meet you, Mary—then she squeezed Mary's hand spasmodically as a fresh wave of pain cascaded through her body. Mary could almost see it.

Meanwhile Doc had removed his overcoat, and he was wearing a college sweater beneath, Presley College, frayed white letters on faded maroon wool—matching his gray suit pants and scuff-toed black shoes only in wear.

This is indelicate, he said, but we need to see what we're doing. He handed his overcoat to Egg, and he and the young Negro held it between them as a curtain of privacy while Doc saw to the girl and the baby's birth. Egg was curious to look over his shoulder but kept his gaze forward, mainly at the radio, whose voice told of Hurricane's continued pounding.

The modicum of privacy allowed the girl to abandon the social context and she began giving inarticulate voice to the pain and fear. Don, without being instructed, brought folded white towels, a roll of gauze, and on top of the stack metal clips and a pair of long-bladed scissors. He delivered them then returned to the counter.

Julie, needing more than Mary's hand, took her by the shoulders and squeezed her to her body. Mary didn't resist. Mary felt Julie's swollen breast against her arm, and Julie's hot, teary breath on her cheek with each agonized crying out.

You're doing great, just great—and Mary wanted to trust her own words but sensed their betrayal, like a villainous actor patient in the wings.

There's the crown, push now, young lady, push. . . .

And agony's fiery breath was upon Mary's cheek.

Egg noticed that the Negro's eyes concentrated forward, like his own, but he winced slightly at each crying out, and sweat rolled from beneath his cap and spilled along the bones of his dark face like the paths of tears. Egg heard Mary cooing comfort to the girl and he knew their strange coming here was the Lord's work, but also that funny-sounding word in Mrs. Wilson's class: *serendipity*.

The diner's door opened, and a man rushed in, Doc's age, perhaps older, definitely shorter, paunchier. The car's right out front, getting warm. Egg realized it was one of the counter-men; in the confusion he hadn't notice him leave. Snow had blown inside with his re-entrance and it fell melting to the floor.

The bell signaled the end of another round, concluding with *a standing eight*, and there was a new cry in the diner. Doc was at work with the scissors. Egg glanced over his shoulder at the scissors' clicking but Doc's body shielded his view.

In a moment Egg's job was done. The counter-man lifted up the Negro girl as easily as a sack of grain; the girl clutched a bloody bundled towel to her chest. It was decided instantly, almost as if scripted beforehand, that Doc and

Mary would ride with the girl and baby, and Egg would follow with the boy in his truck.

Mary took Egg's jacket from their booth. Everything was happening quickly. Egg touched her arm. After this, we're going home, right?

You can go if you need to, Egg.

But, Mary-Mary, surely all this . . .

It's a sign?

Something like that.

There's balance in the world, Egg—in the *cosmos*.

They'd been rushing too and they stepped outside, suddenly in the storm.

Balance? lifting his voice above the cold white wind.

One baby born on this day—

Egg felt no desire to complete the equation as he watched Mary slide into the passenger seat of the wide rumbling Mercury, and pull closed its heavy door.

The new father was at Egg's side waiting to be led to his truck.

They turned away from the wind, and snow fell like grains of stars in the city lights . . . beyond which were the black and silence of night.

Scent of Darkness

Scent of Darkness

What is essential is invisible to the eye
—Antoine de Saint-Exupéry

Scene 1

It'd been Rhonda Holcomb's idea to approach Mrs. Espejo about directing the Passion. It was Bob Abernathy's turn to direct but something was going on with Mr. Abernathy. There were rumors he sat in his basement every night smoking and tinkering with his model airplanes until the small hours of the night (model-size packages did arrive by post once a week or more, that was confirmed by several). Then Mrs. Abernathy spoke to the mayor, over spears of broccoli at Wilson's Grocery, and told him Bob wouldn't be able to direct the Passion. No one was quite sure what to do; no one had ever forfeited the opportunity to direct. But Rhonda Holcomb felt it her duty to solve the dilemma since David was to play a leading role—and her husband was looking forward to it so. The Espejo woman, Carmelita, had moved to the village the previous fall, by herself, and purchased the old Johnson place. She was a widow, apparently, who'd come from back east. She always wore black or white—something that called attention to her dark features, by complement or contrast. Rumor had it she was nearly fifty but the foreignness of her look made it difficult to say. Mrs. Espejo came to church every Sunday, and she said her good-mornings to Pastor Phillips and the other congregants, but she sat alone in the farthest pew. People claimed she was working a rosary, praying silently—but if she was Catholic she could go to church in Crawford: In fact, why hadn't she moved *there*?

So here stood Mrs. Holcomb on the widow's gray-painted porch (the gray had begun to peel), on a Thursday morning, with a pan of monkey-bread, turning the bell-key. Perhaps Mrs. Espejo wasn't at home. The others thought Rhonda was daft when she suggested the widow. It might bring her into the community more, to be part of something important. Yes, they said, but directing the Passion? She's from back east—she must know a thing or two about plays.

Mrs. Espejo answered the door, seeming only mildly surprised to see Rhonda Holcomb. Perhaps she'd been expecting a visit of some sort. Up close, the widow wasn't as darkly featured as Rhonda believed, but her hair was black, truly black (no one else in the village had truly black hair, not even Mrs. Wilson, who was known to dye hers); and the widow's eyes, which rested on high round cheekbones, were of a liquid brown that seemed to seep into you, the way the juice of a hickory nut can and stain your skin for months. The widow was in a black dress but Rhonda wondered if it was in fact a dress of mourning—it was too lacy about the collar, and the cuffs were too pretty. Maybe it was merely a style that the widow preferred, something she'd acquired back east. Maybe Carmelita Espejo wasn't a widow at all.

Scene 2

At coffee and cards, in Mrs. Reynolds's kitchen, the other wives were anxious to hear what'd happened. Rhonda gave a disappointingly brief report. Mrs. Espejo agreed to direct—she enjoyed local theater—and she looked forward to reading the script. Jean Reynolds had stopped pouring coffee to hear the news. After a moment's pause she returned to pouring.

Rhonda could've said more. She could've said how the widow was dressed. She could've commented on the inside of her house: the hallway's bookcases brimming with books whose spines spoke of biology and anatomy; the kitchen with its shelves of unique utensils and unnamable gadgets, and more books, these with a foreign language upon their covers, possibly French or Italian; the curtains of heavy black velvet which must've shut out every morsel of light when drawn; the table and chairs of darkest wood that were as fancy as the architecture of old buildings; the fact that the widow pressed her coffee instead of percolating it, and the beans were as black as the curtains, as black as her hair; the widow sweetened her cup with cinnamon instead of sugar; and served the monkey-bread on china as light as the steam rising from the fragrant coffee. Rhonda might've mentioned that the whole time, the widow smiled like the martyrs in the old paintings that she'd seen in a book at the library. Like she was both doomed and blessed.

And she could've said she wasn't certain the widow was a widow at all.

But Rhonda felt a sort of uneasy possessiveness about Mrs. Espejo, a woman at least ten years her senior. She wanted these observations and impressions for herself, for the time being anyway. Thus she left her friends with the mystery of her visit, and the widow's easy agreement to direct the Passion.

—

Scene 3

David's costume was hanging in the breezeway. Mrs. Perkins said it'd been dry-cleaned, up in Crawford, after her husband had worn it the previous year, but it didn't smell quite right to Rhonda, so she hoped a good airing would help. The sun was already low, low enough to drop below the treeline of Hollis Woods, and the Holcombs' backyard was in a kind of twilight. Against that backdrop, the Plague costume took on an especially sinister character. Three years before, the costume gave the Jones children nightmares so Mrs. Jones returned it to the church's storeroom, and there it stayed between rehearsals. No doubt Mrs. Jones was pleased when the Passion was performed and the costume was no longer their responsibility.

She knew it was ridiculous but Rhonda began to feel that the empty eyes of the mask, with its glossy black beak, were looking at her. She wished that she'd hung the costume so that the headpiece and mask faced the darkening yard.

A noise inside the house, David or Davey, Jr., startled Rhonda and she felt silly—there was nothing to fear in the lifeless costume. To assure herself of her ease she stepped forward and reached out to touch one of the costume's plumed arms—the plumage was fashioned from black felt and lay in evenly staggered layers. Rhonda expected the winglike arm to feel cool, as cool as the breeze moving freely through the room, but the feathers were warm to Rhonda's touch, and the sensation was as disquieting as the look from the fathomless eye-holes.

She quickly took the costume by its shoulders and turned it on its wire hanger to face the yard. It was suspended from clothesline that stretched across the breezeway near the ceiling. Rhonda's agitated motion made Plague bounce on the line. She glanced back before entering the kitchen, and the enlivened costume appeared to be laughing, silently but mirthfully, as the feathers quivered in the quiet air.

Scene 4

The Passion would take place on the village square, with the gazebo as a part of the staging area, but only the last rehearsal or two would take place there. Otherwise the players practiced in the church basement, and some wooden pallets served as the approximated gazebo.

Mrs. Espejo was a few minutes late to the first rehearsal, which made the actors uneasy—though they attempted not to display it, too plainly, out of deference to Rhonda, who'd come to show her support as she didn't have a role in the play. Or perhaps it was out of deference to David, whom everyone in the village liked. He was a tall, even-tempered man who wasn't quick with a joke but he'd laugh along easily with others. He supervised the bins just south of the village but he'd learned carpentry skills from his father and there were few projects he couldn't handle. In fact, the one man in the village who occasionally had an unkind word regarding David Holcomb was George Dickson, the carpenter, as sometimes David's generosity in assisting his neighbors was money out of George's pocket.

But Mrs. Espejo arrived with the mimeographed copy of the Passion in her handbag—apologizing for being late, with that martyr's smile on her lips—and Rhonda noticed that the script had numerous notes and markings as the widow took it from her bag and the pages fanned open for a moment. Mrs. Espejo was in black, but it was silky, certainly not the coarse cotton of Rhonda's everyday dresses, Rhonda's and the other women's in the village. Rhonda wondered if Mrs. Espejo dressed as she did to stand apart, deliberately, if her efforts to make the widow more at home in the village were pointless, if the last thing the widow wanted was to be at home here. Still, she'd accepted the task of directing the Passion. . . .

The widow had settled into a folding chair (Rhonda brought her a cup of coffee and apologized that there was no cinnamon), and the players introduced themselves and their roles. Then Mrs. Espejo directed them to do their first read-through. It was a term not used, specifically, and it seemed to bolster their confidence in the widow, and in Rhonda for having thought of her. The narrator was *Otto Mueller*, who spoke of coming to the village originally. *Mueller* had retrieved the old battered suitcase (more like a trunk) from the storeroom, and it was on the floor next to his folding chair. *Otto Mueller* listed the name of every family in the village—there were far fewer then—but before he completed the list, Mrs. Espejo stopped him. Let's shorten the list. We'll have the Endicotts of course, but as it is now they are lost in the list. Also, I'm not certain the German accent is necessary. It's Bavarian; the Muellers were from Bavaria. I think the case and the clothes will communicate your foreignness. These are my clothes. Doesn't everyone already know the story? David spoke up, Mrs. Espejo has a point—try it without the accent, George. Maybe we'll prefer it, and it'll be easier, won't it? That accent must be hard to keep up for the entire play.

It went on that way, with the widow cutting and rearranging lines and even whole scenes, meanwhile paraphrasing new ones to be written in. The players became more and more used to it—not accepting of it precisely. It was just that Mrs. Espejo's opinions were difficult to resist: There was the beatific smile and the calm but steady advance that took no real notice of objections; plus revisions were sweetened with a sprinkling of sugar—no, not sugar, *that* was too sweet . . . cinnamon.

Rhonda watched it all from a folding chair in the basement, near the choir director's blue-painted desk, and by the end of the evening she wasn't quite certain what'd happened. She'd never seen anyone manage a group as the widow had. The Passion, which had been performed in the village for generations with little change, had been systematically dissected and revised by the widow's directorial vision.

Scene 5

What do you think? Rhonda was spooning coffee into the percolator basket while David, seated at the kitchen table, was beginning to pick through the newspaper for items he hadn't read. They'd come home from the read-through, Rhonda checked on Davey to make sure he'd done his homework, and they decided they wanted coffee even though it was well into the evening. Actually David had wanted coffee, and Rhonda decided to make enough for herself too.

What do you think? she repeated. David seemed well into his paper already.

About?

The widow, the play—any of it. Rhonda fitted the basket over the metal stem, submerged the stem in the pot, secured the lid and plugged the percolator into the socket next to the sink.

Still looking at his paper. She seemed nice. He turned a page. His reading glasses were halfway down his nose, something that had always irritated Rhonda, a little, but she had an urge to step over to the table and push David's glasses squarely onto his face.

What about all the changes?

David didn't respond for a moment. Then as he was turning a page, he looked at Rhonda above his glasses. You wanted to bring her in.

The water heating in the percolator began to vibrate the pot on the counter.

David returned his attention to the paper, whose news was already old.

Scene 6

It seemed to absorb the dark of night so that in dawn's twilight it appeared more than merely black but an actual void, an emptiness in the air that one might step through into another place altogether, like Alice's rabbit-hole. Somehow its eyes were blacker still, a deeper depth of emptiness, so that their blackness stood apart, watching, like the eyes of a marine creature staring back from its alien world. Its plumage fluttered briefly, animating the void, almost beckoning one closer, making one wonder if the absorbed night made it colder to the touch—the opposite of a black thing's taking in sunlight all day. Would the concentrated cold of night burn too?

David stepped into that cold and wore it easily, and perhaps the coldness lingered on his skin, and the scent of darkness too.

Scene 7

It was brought upon the land by the native peoples, the Chicahoga and their kin the Siwash, and Plague lurked in dark caves and riverbeds—until the Founders arrived to establish this peaceloving Christian community on the edge of the devil's woods.

I know that's the legend, but . . .

It's more than a legend. That's the way it was. It's been passed on, verbatim, to each generation. *Otto Mueller*, appropriately, had become the spokesman for the players. He was a simple schoolteacher who taught the *First Children* rocks and minerals, algebra, leaf identification, George

Washington, Annabel Lee, and Macbeth.

That's why I'd been letting it pass, because of its sacredness, but . . .

They stared at her, dressed in black and white, with a gray houndstooth scarf looped loosely about her neck. Mrs. Hulbertson, the choir director, sat at the piano bench, turned so she could watch the drama; and Rhonda sat upon a cold folding chair near Mrs. Hulbertson. The drama had halted rehearsal.

It's just . . . well, there's really no basis for it. In scientific fact, I mean.

Otto Mueller pushed back his hat, its brim black and perfectly circular, revealing a thick-cheeked face that was perfectly perplexed. The other players, and Mrs. Hulbertson and Rhonda, too, were at an equal loss, but they allowed their perplexity to channel through Otto Mueller, whose cheeks were flushing crimson in the basement's close air. The piano bench squeaked beneath Mrs. Hulbertson's shifting weight.

I think . . . (the voice seemed to emit from nowhere) . . . I think what Mrs. Espejo is saying (it was David speaking from behind the crow-faced mask—even Rhonda couldn't place the queerly muffled voice at first) . . . is that it's like Mr. Washington's cherry tree (David's voice had an alien quality, as if he truly were part crow, a sort of cawing lilt, a ragged, high-pitching trail at the end of each phrase). We know now that he never chopped down the tree—but George—our George—is right too: the story's been said so often that it's become true. In fact, it becomes truer every time it's spoken (*spo-caawwwn*).

Everyone was looking at Plague, intended to be a dumb-player. David's eyes, always almost violet in their blueness, suddenly seemed gray to Rhonda. The mask shaded and darkened them—she hadn't noticed before.

For all the wisdom of Plague's speech, it wasn't clear where that left the lines. Rhonda knew, though, the widow would have her way. That'd been the truth from the beginning.

Scene 8

Rhonda wore the black nightgown to bed, the one that slipped over her head and had the three unnecessary buttons at the wide neck, like a peasant's blouse. She left the buttons undone as she came into the bedroom, where David was already in bed. He was lying on his back, covers drawn up, his eyes shut against the lamplight coming from Rhonda's nightstand. He wasn't asleep, Rhonda could tell. Rhonda slipped into bed. So what was the problem with the widow's lock? She was sitting up, and she'd angled her shoulders slightly, so that the top of her nightgown fell open.

David didn't respond for a moment. A pin in the handle assembly broke. His eyes remained closed. His voice was monotone, lifeless.

Is that strange? Rhonda shifted her weight so that her hip pressed against his elbow. David wore a white undershirt and pajama pants.

It happens—eyes still closed, so that he couldn't see that Rhonda was wearing the nightgown, that the buttons were left undone.

Rhonda switched off the lamp and scooted beneath the covers. After a moment, Rhonda's finger grazed David's left thigh. A few leg hairs poked through the flannel of his pajamas. David breathed as if he was sleeping.

Rhonda thought of putting her head on his shoulder, her hand on his chest, her fingertips near his nipple, but before she could decide he rolled away from her on his side. She imagined that soon he truly would be asleep, and she would have no choice but to slip her hand between her thighs, to stroke her need for him . . . to solace her need to know.

Scene 9

Rhonda woke in the night. The noise hadn't roused her suddenly but rather it'd been part of her dream world—it had begun there then migrated upward, outward, into the real world—and she followed it, the crowsong, from the depths of sleep to full wakefulness. She lay in bed trying to locate the cawing.

Surely it was outside, coming from the trees that picketed the yard. But crows didn't croak their song to the moon like nightingales. Besides, it didn't seem to emit from outdoors. Rhonda pulled off the covers and placed her feet on the floor. The wood felt cold and a trifle gritty—housework had suffered. She slipped from her room and padded along the silent hall, silent except for the cawing, which was coming from downstairs. She'd known its source even while dreaming.

Her feet were careful on each step, and she didn't bother switching on a livingroom lamp while she walked through the dark downstairs. The kitchen still smelled of potato soup. Then she stood in the breezeway's entrance.

Plague was turned toward the backyard, deeply shadowed in lunarlight. He called out his cawing song more than sang it. Perhaps it echoed in the tree-lined yard, or something out there was responding in dark kind. After a moment he must've sensed Rhonda's presence. He turned to her slowly, not troubling to flap his black-wing arms.

Why have you caawwwm? His voice both rough and shrill.

Rhonda was oddly calm, in the dark, with Plague a black crowshaped shadow against the barely moonlit yard.

That is my question: Why have you come? Are we ill, my family and I?

Plague was silent. He tilted his plumed head for a moment. Have you caawwwse?

Does illness have a cause, beyond the nature of illness itself?

Hesitation. You are caawwwlm.

Hesitation. Yes.

Plague moved his head and upperbody crowlike. Why? I know you.

You know Death?

Rhonda recalled a catalogue of deaths: her parents', seven years apart, her grandparents', also seven years apart, her uncle's, crushed beneath a tractor, a distant cousin's, suffocated in a grain bin, friends'. That's not what I mean.

Plague stared at her, his glossy black beak catching angles of moonlight.

There was an old sofa in the breezeway. Rhonda thought of sliding out of her underpants and pulling off the nightgown, letting it fall to the invisible floor, knowing her skin would glow cadaverously—then lying on the sofa, beckoning Plague's black cock inside her, perhaps even taking him so that his dark head nestled in her throat—a sensation she'd only known once and had secretly wanted since. . . .

A noise behind Rhonda drew her attention.

Mom? What're you doing? Davey Jr. was in the kitchen rubbing his eyes. His pajama pants were too long and he stood on their cuffs.

Nothing. Let's get you back to bed.

She went to Davey, turned him around by the shoulders and led him from behind, back through the house and upstairs, into his room. Davey was nearly as tall as his mother, so she watched their progress just beyond the crewcut crown of his head.

Just before they reached the second floor, Rhonda thought she heard the front door of the house open and quickly shut, but with their noisy creaking on the old stairs it was difficult to be sure. She waited in Davey's room while he drank some water from a glass on his nightstand. Then he said he'd forgotten his prayers, so he got beneath the covers, put his hands together and thanked God for the people in his life, one by one, and asked for their protection. In the corner a nightlight of Baby Jesus in Mary's arms glowed wanly.

Meanwhile, Rhonda stood on the cold floor listening acutely for other out-of-place sounds. There were none. She touched Davey's cheek and left him nodding off.

In her own room, in the dark, Rhonda saw the landscape of blankets on David's side of the bed. She quietly took her spot, now cold, and reached over to discover if his side was occupied. It was. She felt the thigh and knee. He said nothing but perhaps was awake. Rhonda rolled away from him and listened to the house's darkness.

Scene 10

Mrs. Espejo's house was old and had had many occupants—a combination for disrepair. There was a leaky fitting in the basement, the flue in the parlor fireplace was sticky, as was a window in an upstairs bedroom, and floorboards moaned annoyingly in nearly every room.

Your husband is a godsend, Mrs. Holcomb.

Rhonda, please. Yes, David's handy to be sure.

She and the widow were in the church basement watching while the Passion's cast carried props and odds and ends from the storeroom. Everything was being transported to the square, where they would have one full rehearsal before the next day's performance. The rehearsal would take place from four to six while twilight fell. It was understood that the village folk would avoid the square for those two hours so that nothing would be spoiled for the performance. Rumors had spread, void of particulars, that the widow had insisted on significant alterations to the traditional script.

Will you have people at the play?

People?

Yes, any family or friends, from back home?

No, my people are too far away—besides, there's almost no one anyway.

That's a shame.

The widow smiled, not quite the smile of martyrdom, merely sad.

Rhonda felt a twinge of something. Not sympathy—in fact quite the opposite. She felt a pang of glee, but not at Mrs. Espejo's solitariness, rather, that her interest in David was just a matter of wanting company—the sound of someone banging about in the basement, fixing stubborn flues, adjusting joists. A human body nearby to displace some emptiness for a while. David wasn't the sort to be unfaithful. Now Rhonda's happiness faded to guilt, for being suspicious, for assuming the worst.

I think that's it, said David from the basement stairs.

O/O k/k, the women said simultaneously.

Ok, repeated David then turned and climbed the steps.

Scene 11

The ticking of their bedroom clock could sometimes be a comfort, a reliable pulse in the heart of their home, but when Rhonda woke in the middle of the night, the ticking was a metronomic reminder that morning was coming on and the time for precious sleep was fading with every metallic tink. She lay on her side listening to the clock, across the room on the bureau, and after a long while she reached back to feel David's body . . . but there was nothing except bedclothes. Her hand groped the twists of blanket and sheet for a moment. She sat up and David's absence was clear even in the darkened room. Perhaps it was his leaving that woke her.

Rhonda rose and in the hall she paused for a moment at Davey's half-open door until she heard the gentle rumble of his sleep breathing. The house felt cold, and to her bare feet the wood was icy. There was no climatic reason for this sudden wintry chill. Rhonda checked the downstairs rooms and even the basement, only to confirm what she knew already: David was not there.

Her checking concluded in the breezeway, where hung the reflection of this strange David, the man she didn't know. Perhaps it was due to the cold air moving through the house but Plague turned to her on his wire hanger, slowly, and his empty eyes met hers.

Rhonda waited for Plague to speak. He only rotated back and forth, slowly, like a sometime-ago hanged man— the sort that crows would pick at.

She knew that she had to go out. She thought of the outdoors as chilled as inside her house . . . inside her bones. She slid off her nightgown and underpants, leaving them in a heap, and took Plague from the clothesline. Working in the dark, she unbuttoned the plumed suit and took the black pants from the hanger. She laid the suit and head on the old sofa while she stepped into the pants and gently pulled them up, the velveteen material whispering along her calves before the smooth seam kissed the insides of her thighs, intensifying the tingle that had begun the moment she touched Plague on his hanger. She had to pull the pants nearly to her chest for their crotch to nip into her with just the perfect amount of pain.

She took up the plumed suit and worked her arms into

the seraphic sleeves. Her nipples, already raised from the house's cold, turned to stones at the touch of Plague upon her white breasts. She slowly buttoned the suit, feeling it squeeze her breasts together. She wiggled against the biting crotch and seemed to hear Plague's whispering caw close at her ear, a pointed tongue, ripe with carrion scent, running along its delicate rim. The whispering grew more heated suggesting the placement of the pointed tongue elsewhere, everywhere . . . as her feathered hands lifted up the mask and headpiece. She had been thinking of pulling on the final parts slowly, savoring the sensation, but she couldn't resist the urge to plunge her head inside, and as she opened her eyes to Plague's viewing the shattering crashed through her taut body, weakening her knees and making the breeze-way roll as if in a seismic eruption.

Scene 12

The Johnson place had grown wild since the widow moved into it. She'd hired a boy now and then to mow the grass but the shrubs and trees had gone untended, to the point where there'd been gossiping complaints among the village folk. The overgrowth made it easy to perch close to the house unseen, to be a darkness among the dark things of the yard.

The house was lighted here and there, an upstairs window faintly, the kitchen, and perhaps the downstairs hall. Though its style was commonplace in the village, with its muntined windows and Queen Anne traces, the house seemed now of another land—foreign, forced and even slightly grotesque. As unnatural on the block as a sand crane, as unwholesome as spoiled milk.

Wind cut through the overgrowth and insects scissored every so often, but otherwise the village was as quiet as a careful thief.

For a long while there was no activity. The quarter-moon rose into a viewing spot among the branches then floated beyond it, followed by an indigo wisp of cloud.

The door opened.

Lemon-colored light from the hall spilled onto the porch creating a candescent corridor for *David* to walk through, the old red toolbox in his hand his only prop. *Carmelita* stepped into the corridor. Thank you, said her quiet voice. My pleasure, said his. He turned at the edge of the light and stepped back toward her. The yellow intensified to white spotlight to capture the lovers' kiss. Blinding.

When the blindness faded, the porch was empty and dark. The house was dark, its here-and-there lights extinguished as if by a single motion. The dark place of the yard desired to bleed into the darkness that was everywhere, as if a curtain was closing.

THE PASSION

(Otto Mueller, suitcase in hand, enters and looks all around, seeing new sights. He goes to the top step of the gazebo, turns.)

Otto: It lurked in damp caves and riverbeds . . . until the Founders arrived to establish this peaceloving Christian community on the edge of the woods.

(The First Children, five in all, enter one by one, sit Indian-style, and direct their eager attention to Mr. Mueller.)

Otto: The good people worked hard taming the prairie, building the village, studying the Bible, and teaching the children.

Child One: We learned numbers, addition, subtraction, multiplication, division, and even algebra and geometry.

Child Two: We learned reading, spelling and punctuation.

Child Three: We learned history, about Mr. Washington, Mr. Jefferson and Mr. Lincoln.

Child Four: We learned about growing food and keeping animals, cows, pigs, horses, sheep and chickens.

Child Five: We learned the Scripture and about Jesus' love and how the Plague took the firstborn sons . . . and how Plague was driven into the wilderness and waited for the children of God.

(Plague comes from behind the gazebo, moving his wings as if in flight, takes Child One and leads him to the other side of the gazebo, out of view, completing a circle. The other children are panicked and sad. They whimper.)

Otto: Plague took the firstborn to begin but soon seized upon whole families. *(Plague appears again. Father and Mother and two Other Children, all wearing faces of mourning, come from the crowd and Plague directs them to go in a line behind the gazebo.)* Then neighbors were taken. *(Two more Families rise and walk sadly away.)* Plague was rapacious. *(Plague follows behind flapping his wings excitedly.)* We prayed for deliverance from the scourge.

(Otto Mueller takes the hands of congregants [audience members] near him, the congregants clasp hands, then Otto begins leading them in prayer [Psalm 23]. Plague appears in the gazebo silently watching the congregants pray. Jesus the

Redeemer appears next to Plague smiling benevolently at the congregants. The prayer ends . . . save for one voice which continues repeating 'Surely goodness and love will follow me all the days of my life, Surely goodness and love will follow me all the days of my life,' etc.)

Wife: Surely goodness and love will follow me all the days of my life, Surely goodness and love will follow me all the days of my life, Surely . . .

(Congregants stare at the Wife, uncertain of her breaking of the Passion. She continues, all the while staring up at Plague. Jesus the Redeemer appears bewildered. His smile fades from benevolence to veiled confusion.)

Plague: *(Stepping forward.)* What are you doing? Caaaawlm down.

(The Wife continues repeating, then turns to the Widow.)

Widow: *(Standing.)* Stop. You're ruining everything.

(The Wife pauses for an instant . . . then returns to the phrase.)

Congregant: What's the meaning of this?

(On the gazebo, Plague removes his mask and headpiece. Beneath, his face is scarlet. Jesus the Redeemer scratches at his patchy beard.)

The Drama of Consonants

The Drama of Consonants

Only then attempt to win by force

—Niccolò Machiavelli

We say, it was springtime and the honeysuckle hummed with bees; and the bees and the blossoms were so close in color that from a distance one could forget about the honeybees' suckling and believe the bush itself was ahum—a newfangled electric bush like they may have up in Crawford one day, the way things are going. No thank you. Oil lamps work just fine, and fuel for the stove never runs low, not with Hollis Woods right here, sitting on the village's shoulder. And busting a field behind Old Bob's pulling, handchurning, walking to worship on the Sabbath . . . these keep a body fit. Old Man Stevenson lived to a hundred-and-one and danced a right proper reel on his hundred-and-first.

The wind was hard and biting—it whipped the heavy canvas—and more than one voice was heard *Praise Lord* before they could see it wasn't an O'Brien but merely the whipping wind. They counted the offerings left before the O'Briens' door *one, two, three* and the men spoke of the wind, above it. If it didn't subside it wouldn't be safe for the burning. But burn we must. After a time they disbursed to go about their day. Except James Reynolds, who lingered longer than the rest.

Mr. O'Brien had been seen at an upstairs window—or perhaps it was his spirit, looking down upon Willow Street a final time. He was as pale and thin as one of Pastor Anthony's wafers; and he wore an expression of profound sadness: The same one he'd worn when Elizabeth's little brother had been lost to the whooping cough. All through the funeral and burial Bob O'Brien leaned on his wife and on Elizabeth, literally much of time. Elizabeth was only eleven then, no, she'd just turned twelve—but she seemed a grown woman in her mourning dress, cutting white cake for the visitors, smiling bravely beneath her high cheekbones while her father more than once had to retreat to the church's kitchen to breakdown in private. He, or his spirit, looked upon Willow Street, masked in that same pale sadness . . . perhaps Bob O'Brien had lost another child.

At Wilson's Grocery, Mrs. Wilson reached beneath the counter and removed a paper bag. Even after forty years—eight working for the widower Mr. Wilson, a pigtailed girl right out of school, and thirty-two married to Mr. Wilson—Susan still noticed the scent of the brown paper, as heavy as the bags themselves. She unfolded and opened it on the countertop. She pushed the glasses higher on her nose, beyond the bridge, and put her face over the newly opened bag, where the scent would be the strongest. . . . There were the usual things to place inside: the bouillon cubes and crackers, the peanuts and wedges of dried apples and apricots, the black tea, also the gauze and bandage clips, the salve, the peroxide, the iodine, the aspirin tablets. She was alone in the store. Susan watched the door, only a few feet from the counter. She looked at the string attached to the door and followed with her eyes as it threaded up and through hooks to a bell whose tinny jingle marked the entrance or exit of a customer. The bell was silent. Who was to know? . . . if she shorted the O'Briens a few cubes of bouillon, a half handful of nuts, a strip or two of gauze, a clip or two for bandages? She and Mr. Wilson weren't losing any money. On the contrary, shrewd Mr. Wilson quoted the Council full prices, and perhaps then some, and the councilmen approved the expenditure—it would've been political sacrilege to balk at the cost of the O'Brien family's tragedy. No, it wasn't the money. It was the waste . . . all that good food especially, God's bounty, perishing in the flames. This was the fourth bag after all; it would be placed on their porch alongside the other three, untouched. No one believed the O'Briens were alive in there. Bob O'Brien's ghost had been seen, hadn't it? Surely there would be a burning—so this steady wind must abate before the fifth day's end.

There were rumblings in the village, about the burning, about whether it should be done—not because of the dry west wind that rattled every awning, and made metal mailbox flags clank against their boxes like overexcited telegraphers—but rather it'd become antiquated. It'd been more than a decade since the Mesmores: *Perhaps we should leave the burnings to the past. Science after all. . . .* Science! Beau Bishop had no patience for it. He'd seen plenty of science in the trenches *the Vicker's, the Kaiser's null-acht, the flamethrower.* His sweat still smelled of mustard, and he was among the lucky. The talkers—whisperers really—they needed to go sit in the gazebo, read the names painted in gold, and speak to the dead, tell them that these days their sacrifice no longer counts. Their abiding by the rule for the good of the village, for their friends and neighbors—well, it no longer matters because of *Science.* Beau Bishop decided that some of them required watching, like that Reynolds boy, James. He hadn't said anything, as far as Beau knew, but the gossip was he was sweet on the O'Brien girl, Elizabeth; and boys in love can become excitable and do funny things. Yes, James Reynolds needed watching, him, and the whisperers.

The crow-shaped weathervane on Stevenson's barn spun madly but always showed a west wind when the chaos held it steady for a moment. *Zeff* they called this wind when he was a boy. Beware Zeff, he'll bring flood and draught, famine and wildfire. Worst of all lightning without rain and almost without warning, bolts that hit like blasts out of a bruise-blue sky, just as if hurled down by the angry Jehovah of Second Samuel. Some said if a burning was required, let God's hand do the firing, let Him call upon Zeff and send a white-hot bolt to the house of the stricken, burning it to ash along with the dead inside. But God was rarely so direct and required the hand of man to do His will. This time though . . . Zeff's forward guard had been so persistent . . . perhaps this burning would not call upon the hand of man, and skeptics would find their place in the silent dark.

Margaret Olstetter sat in her front porch's swing, her schoolbooks strapped in a stack at her side, and she listened to her father's wheezy coughing through the barely open window of the room he called his study, though mainly he just read his papers in there, and sipped his daddy's coffee, which was brewed strong and sweetened from the brown bottle he kept in a recess of the kitchen cabinet, up high where she and her mother had difficulty reaching. Margaret was sick to her stomach. She could see the O'Brien house from her porch, just two blocks west, on the opposite side of Willow Street. She imagined Elizabeth and how she couldn't have known, not for certain, perhaps not at all, when the final time was that she was entering her home, when the councilmen and Mayor Bishop would tell the O'Briens they were sorry but they could not leave their house, then Mr. Holcomb and some of the other men built the portal out of old boards and heavy canvas painted red. Margaret watched the blood-red canvas shudder in the wind, the warm wind that chilled her as she sat on her porchswing, terrified to walk inside. Maybe as terrified as Elizabeth was. Margaret's father coughed and turned his newspaper page. Margaret shifted her gaze back to the O'Briens' and was surprised to see a figure standing on the walk before the house, just standing motionless, a gray sweater and darker gray trousers. Mr. O'Brien's ghost? Margaret had heard her father and mother talking—people had seen Mr. O'Brien here and there in the village, haunting it, perhaps searching for a child to replace his own. What was the little boy's name? No, this figure wasn't Mr. O'Brien, unless death had made him taller and leaner, and grown out his hair full and black: It was James there on the walk, as silent as a spirit. If Margaret were shut up in her house, would a boy come to moon at her windows? Patrick perhaps or Daniel? Liam? All the boys took notice of Elizabeth, tall and slender and emerald-eyed, even the boys' fathers, but Margaret's hair was mousy, her complexion uneven, and every room she entered she entered unnoticed. She suddenly felt lonely, too, afraid and lonely.

Mr. Oliver talked of the power of language. He diagramed sentences in bold white strokes of chalk *verb, adjective, preposition, gerund, infinitive.* The sleeves of his wool jacket became dusty with the force of language. And his voice, trained under the name of Sergeant Oliver, filled the words of the poets like boiler-born steam. *Hiawatha, Sun-Down Poem, Much Madness, Annabel Lee.* That was the one that inhabited James. Though the image of the sounding sea was pure theory, its waves battered at his brain with cruel persistence, as steady as the metronome

Mr. Oliver used to teach the rhythm of the lines. And the chilling nightwind chilled him to the core, blowing out of a cloud that covered his soul, casting everything in darkness. But it was the image of the dead maiden that haunted him most profoundly. She had come to him on the first night speaking quiet words of Elizabeth, words he could only half hear, quarter comprehend. The maiden's cadaverous skin glowed in the darkness that surrounded his soul, her eyes like blue flames fluttering on the cusp of extinction, her yellow hair flecked with graveyard dirt. She wouldn't leave him even come morning but stayed at his shoulder adding her nonsensical words to the battering sea and chilling wind. Never-ceasing, like the real wind that'd been blowing through the village for days. He hoped the maiden might take up with the spirit of Mr. O'Brien, giving ghostly comfort to one another and letting him be.

Beau Bishop stood outside Owens' Café a moment before going in. The mayor tried to sense some abatement in the wind, some hint it was slowing and would slow enough to silence the skeptics about the burning. The wind added fuel to their fire that the fire shouldn't proceed—for the safety of the entire village, they'd say, leaving out the part that they were opposed on principle already. Rabblerousers, agitators. It was their kind in Europe that started the whole mess, that got him and his brothers dragged into the infernal trenches over there. Beau needed to see who exactly was saying what exactly. He hitched up the straps on his dungarees, a nervous habit, and entered the café. There were the usual greetings *Mr. Mayor, Hey, Beau, Morning Mayor*, but there was also a noticeable lulling in the babble of conversations. Owens' was half filled. Dickey was working the counter himself; Dick Junior must be taking the lunchshift today. Marian Olstetter was there, waitressing, as she had for a decade. It seemed odd to the village that

Mrs. Olstetter worked outside her home, leaving Margaret to get herself ready for school, and not seeing Ned off to work at the bins; but no one had ever said anything to her, as far as Beau knew. That's how it begins, the slacking, the weakening of traditions—and then you wind up here, with villagers criticizing a way that'd kept the village safe for generations. (There'd been a boy, too, Margaret's little brother, drowned in the lake—the village had all but forgotten.) Beau placed his hat, a well-used straw fedora with a blue band, on the tree and went to the counter. There was a place between Wilson and Goodpath—so Beau could chat groceries and liveries. As far as he knew, neither Wilson nor Goodpath was an agitator (indeed, a plague house was good for Wilson's business, as the Council knew full well that Ronnie hitched up the prices as much as he dare, so he probably preferred they weren't such rare events). Conversations had gone back to their normal tenor. Men were talking of tractors and old tomcats, of sons and the Mrs.' tarnished silver, of crows in the corn and roosters that refused to crow. Of the wind. Beau thanked Dickey for the cup of coffee he placed in front of him on the counter, then he glanced over his shoulder as the café door blew open . . . apparently Beau hadn't closed it completely. Newspaper pages and uncontrolled cowlicks flapped in the sudden draft. My mistake, he said as he left his stool to shut the door, firmly this time. Before he could do so, another patron walked into the café, as if on a gust of wind. It was the Reynolds kid, James. The mayor and the schoolboy stood facing one another.

Pastor Anthony's wife, Victoria, scooped congealed bacon grease into the frying pan and turned up the burner's heat. She watched as the gelatinous, dun-colored glop began to liquefy and fill the kitchen with its richly cured smell, today almost sickening in its potency. She tried not to think of it but she wondered if that was what flesh did in the flames, turn to a fatty broth as it fell from the muscle and bone. She tried to press the wrinkles out of the skirt of her apron. She was nervous. She looked forward to William having his breakfast and leaving for the church, so that she could go to the gardening shed out back and sneak a cigarette. They said the wives in Crawford smoked in their homes, right at their own kitchen tables. Imagine. Her nerves started at cards two days before. Wanda raised the subject or Betty—it didn't matter which—but it was definitely Sally who said, I think about the family—how do we know five days is enough? What if they're in there improving and just sleeping, getting their strength back—then we set their house ablaze? No one said anything except suit for a long while. Finally, Wanda, glancing to either side as if there was anyone in her house besides the five of them, spoke in a hushed voice. I've been thinking about this wind. What if it's God's sign the burnings are wrong, that we shouldn't take such matters into our own hands? The grease began to bubble so Victoria cracked an egg into the pan, and another, and another. William came into the kitchen and kissed her good morning on the back of the head. He took the coffee pot from the stove, poured himself a cup, then sat with it at the table, where his wife had laid out the paper open to his favorite page, the farm bureau news. For two days she'd wanted to tell him about the conversation, to see what he thought, but there seemed little purpose. She knew his mind: Tradition is tradition. Once you begin monkeying with it, order starts to fall from everything—his sermons were regularly embroidered with the theme. Everything would fall asunder: the home, the government, the church. But didn't the country begin with a revolution, and aren't we *Protest*ants? Victoria spooned grease over the eggs and watched their albumen turn white, flecked with crumbs of bacon left in the grease. William? She hadn't turned to him. He made a sound but was obviously concentrating on his paper. Is there anything about the wind? When it may stop?

Doc Halverson tied on his surgical mask with some difficulty due to the wind. Standing on the walk before the O'Briens', at first Doc turned away from the wind; but soon found that it was easier to face the wind. Once accomplished, he took the crowbar that lay at his feet, the one he'd brought with him, and walked toward the porch. His wife, at home, was a wreck—they had argued every evening as he tried to explain that these daily inspections were necessary. It was his duty as the only physician in the village. Even though it was warm, Doc kept his cotton shirt tightly buttoned at the collar, and he pulled on heavy cowhide gloves as he ascended the porchsteps, the crowbar pressed under his arm. In truth, the risk thrilled him—the disease fascinated him, nearly to the point of wanting to experience it directly, but it was a crazy notion that he wouldn't fully articulate even to himself. It was suicidal, and that was a sin. Perhaps though he might see something at a window, catch some glimpse of the disease. On the porch, the red canvas flapped with mocking vigor. Doc saw the paper bags of supplies left at the O'Briens' door, untouched. He went through the canvas and put his gloved hand upon the knob. By decree the door was to be locked at all times, except to bring inside the supplies (if anyone was able). Carefully, slowly, he turned the knob: the door was bolted. He stepped outside the flapping canvas and began systematically checking the windows with the crowbar, to make certain they were securely closed and latched. He started with the porch's windows, then worked his way around the house. To check the second-floor windows and the attic, Doc called to Holcomb and one of his boys waiting at the walk, and they brought a tall ladder and positioned it beneath the window Doc wanted to inspect. They maneuvered the ladder around the house, from window to window. Doc thanked them through the mask. All were secure. He'd seen no one inside. None of the O'Briens *Mr., Mrs., Elizabeth* stirred at the scrape and thump of the heavy ladder, nor at his crowbar upon the sill. The O'Briens had perished, Doc was certain of it. What would they do though if the terrible wind prevented the burning? They would ask his advice, as the village's doctor, and he had no clue what to tell them.

This longing—that's what adults called it—was consuming him. He thought of her every second. His days at school passed in a fog of her images: The time he retrieved a clean fork for her at lunch when hers had fallen on the floor; she gave him her apple as a thank-you; their friends hooted at the exchange. The time Mrs. Davis made them reading partners; that story about Orpheus; and she helped him with a word he didn't know, *plaintively*, but in a way that didn't make him feel stupid; and on the next page she pretended not to know *purge* so that he could help her. The time she played in the piano recital for morning assembly; her blond hair in a ponytail tied with a pink ribbon; her long, thin fingers, nearly as white as the lace-cuffed blouse, danced over the keys, while her eyes, as green as McCalls' meadow in summer, scanned the notes of that song about moonlight. It was the day that James knew he was in love with Elizabeth O'Brien, that he had been for a long while. Watching her there, in the front of the assembly room, seated at Mrs. Foster's glossy black piano, he realized how long he'd been watching her at school, around the village, at church, always with such intense affection—a way he'd never watched anyone before. So that's what the poets meant: It wasn't just *rhyme* and *meter* and words that begin with the same sound. Elizabeth O'Brien walks in beauty, she truly does.

We say, it was autumn, and Hollis Woods were ablaze with color, color that swirled past the eyes kaleidoscopically, blown by the ceaseless wind, almost dizzying in its brilliance. Fallen leaves banked against buildings like blown snow, and children frolicked as they always had. The piles grew greater and greater, the architecture of leaves grander and grander, because no one could burn them for fear the blaze would get away and reduce the entire village to cinders, perhaps even burn Hollis Woods to nothing but blackened splinters. Up in Crawford, they had machines that pulverized the leaves to brown powder—but better to stay with the old ways. The wind would cease soon, and the burnings could begin.

Throughout the village people prepared for bed and preparation included prayer: for an O'Brien to emerge from their house, for the supplies to disappear, for Mr. O'Brien's ghost to leave our children be, for the O'Briens' suffering to be at an end, for the wind to cease, for the wind to never cease, for Elizabeth to be well, for the Council to let go of the old ways, for there to be a plague house every few years, for the agitators to cease their agitating, the whisperers their whispering, for at least one O'Brien to survive, for a boy to moon over her quarantined house in sunlight and moonlight, for the quarantine to work, for the specter of Plague to pass by this house, invisibly black in the black of night.

He hadn't slept well for days so at last his mind had no choice, and he sank into a profound slumber. There in that depth the whispering grew more intense, her lips close at his ear, the breath of words warm upon his skin. He couldn't open his eyes, in this dream, and light played across his lids aquatically. It seemed to be the voice of the dead maiden but something in its quality reminded him of Elizabeth too. He reached out for her—what he'd only dreamt of doing by day—but her voice was without substance, as bodiless and as penetrating as the ceaseless breeze. The words poured into his ear like the Logos of God, and after minutes or hours he realized they were repeating. Thanks to Mr. Oliver he recognized some of the properties of the repeated words—the rhythm, the connective sounds, the somber mood. It was a poem that the voice whispered into his ear in the aquatic dark, ss's that stabbed like serpent tongues, rr's that rolled together like reunited lovers, vowels that paced plaintively between the drama of consonants. Suddenly awake, James lit the candle by his bed. The dream was already fading. He took a pad and pencil from the nightstand and began recording the maiden's words, flickering in his ear like the candescent light upon the page.

The porchswing swayed with the wind, making the rafters creak as if someone sat there rocking to and fro. At first, only half awake, she thought it was her father—but why would he be up at this hour, leave be sitting in the porchswing? Perhaps another father then? Mr. O'Brien haunting the village in search of a lost child? She pictured him there in the swing on the dark porch, as pale and sad as the moon. She wondered if her father would be so distraught at losing her. Would his spirit wander the village streets hoping to find what lingered of her? That thought occupied her for a long while, while the swing swung mournfully in the night. Then: What if it's the specter of Plague himself who's come to call upon the family? What if it's Plague who sits calmly in the swing as patient as the cycling moon? To the village children, Plague was always depicted as a large crowlike creature, human but yet not. Margaret got up from her small bed and worked her arms into a flannel robe. Her bedroom was warm even with the window cracked and the persistent wind. She padded along the hall, past her parents' room, heard her father's snoring, past her brother's, heard nothing, and crept down the stairs. Her father's study had the aura of being off-limits to her and her mother, but it offered the best view of the porch. She entered the space that smelled precisely of her father and went to the window. From the darkened room, spying through the blinds, she watched the swaying swing, painted a spectral white and moonglowing on the shadowed porch. It appeared empty of course; it was merely the wind that made the old beam wince. Margaret buttoned another button of her robe as she slipped through the front doorway and stepped with bare feet onto the cool porch. She steadied the swing before sitting, leaving a space to her side for whoever may wish to join her there.

Pastor Anthony arranged the slips of paper on his desk, in the small study in his home, pieces of heavy cotton stationery torn evenly into strips. He made certain his fountain pen was filled, which he then set aside. Also on his neatly organized desk was the Bible he used to write his sermons—dogeared and annotated, the leather cover as aged and worn as a favorite saddle. He took his task with literal life-and-death seriousness. The Council had asked him to write a passage to put in the paper bag, some piece of Scripture that would help to heal the O'Briens, or at least comfort them, offer them solace. He would write out several passages and selected the one to go into tomorrow's offering, along with the supplies from Wilson. Why not place all of them in the bag? It seemed that that may disperse the potency of God's Word, water it down, like trying to feed too many people with too little food. And after making his selection he would burn the other slips of paper—even having them in the world seemed to dilute

God's power—thus there were no passages left over from the previous nights. *The people walking in darkness have seen a great light; on those living in the land of the shadow of death a light has dawned* Isaiah 9:2 ~~If a wicked man turns away from all his sin~~ *If a man is righteous and keeps all my decrees and does what is just and right, he will surely live; he will not die* Ezekiel 18:21 *The path of the righteous is like the first gleam of dawn, shining ever brighter till the full light of day* Proverbs 4:18 ~~Do not plot harm against your neighbor, who lives trustfully near you~~ ~~Proverbs 3:29~~ *God performs wonders that cannot be fathomed, miracles that cannot be counted. When he passes, I cannot see him; when he goes by, I cannot perceive him* Job 9:10-11 *Those who know your name will trust in you, for you, Lord, have never forsaken those who seek you* Psalms 9:10 Finished, William Anthony stroked his graying goatee and scratched the itch behind his left ear that never quite went away. He turned the slips of paper face down and mixed their order. In the morning he would select one at random, in essence allowing the Divine Hand to choose the healing passage.

There'd been a good photograph of Elizabeth O'Brien in the church's spring bulletin. She and two other girls were holding baby-booties they'd crocheted and were going to mail to flood victims in the South. Mrs. Bishop was an organized packrat and had every piece of paper that came into the house neatly scrapbooked or filed away. Beau easily found the bulletin, and it lay picture-side up on the seat of his Ford as he drove along County 12 toward Crawford. It was a bustling place, godless for the most part, and surely it had a young girl, blond and thin, who might pass for Elizabeth, under the right circumstances. He felt the bib pocket of his dungarees and the folded bills he kept there.

We say, it was wintertime—a frigid but strangely snowless winter. Day upon day, the sun was a bright, cheerless circle that offered no warmth whatsoever. A north wind penetrated every home, making even the most solidly built feel drafty and cold. People huddled in isolation against its merciless howling, hoping for spring rains to soften the frozen earth. No coat, no matter how thick, could keep out the constant chill. Men warmed their frigid fingers around cups of coffee at Owens' Café, and spoke of the uniqueness of the winter, without end, like the north wind itself.

The tinny bell startled Mrs. Wilson, even though she was expecting an early visitor. Customers, as a rule, rarely came into the store so early. She was gathering items in a corner of the grocery. Hello? The young man was startled too—he hadn't noticed her. On the counter, a paper bag stood upright: clearly Mrs. Wilson was in the process of filling it. She returned to the counter holding a can of condensed milk. May I help you? James, isn't it? He shut the door slowly, assuring that the bell wouldn't make a sound. He had dark circles under his eyes—something she wasn't used to seeing in the face of someone so young. The circles were nearly as gray as the sweater he was wearing. I have something, he said, to place in the sack. He held up a piece of paper folded in thirds like a letter. He stepped toward the counter, where Mrs. Wilson had just placed the can of milk into the bag's open mouth. I'm not sure, the Council is very specific. . . . At that moment the door opened and the bell chimed. It was Pastor Anthony. He too was surprised to see James—the sun hadn't risen, the start of school was still some three hours away. How is everything? He walked past James, whose instinct was to hold his offering out of view. Fine, said Mrs. Wilson. You have it, she added unnecessarily as William Anthony proffered the slip of paper. Job nine, he said, ten and eleven. She took the slip from him. God performs wonders, said Mrs. Wilson. Pastor Anthony smiled—Very good. It pays to study His Word, he said to James in the teachable moment, then exited the store. James and Mrs. Wilson returned their attention to each other, and she held out her hand. *For Elizabeth*, it said on the folded paper, written in awkward teenage boy script. Please, don't read it. She smiled reassuringly as she placed it and the passage from Job inside the bag.

Lucas Jones checked and rechecked the brass fittings, he tapped the glass gauges, he tested the soundness of the wheels, he forced water through the large and small hoses looking for leaks: The Merriweather steam-pumper was fit as a fiddle . . . and hopefully wouldn't be needed. Old Bob would pull the Merriweather and water tank into place. The men would transport the aerial ladder in a wagon, along with the axes and shovels. The steam engine would quickly bring the pressure to capacity. (They say up in Crawford their pumpers are motorized, with one motor to power the pumper itself, and one to power the pump. That'd be something to see.) The Council would supply the kerosene, should it be necessary. Lucas stepped out of the fire shed, wetted his finger, and held it in the air, where the wind quickly dried it. He looked back at Miss Mary and wondered if she'd be enough.

Wanda Holcomb selected the hymns *Return O Wanderer to Thy Home, Unclean of Life and Heart Unclean, The Winds Were Howling over the Deep, Rock of Ages, Thou Lord Art a Shield for Me, Come Divine Interpreter, The Great Redeeming Angel Thee, By the Holy Hills Surrounded* and placed torn slips of paper to mark the pages. Five hymnals all together: Eric, Marian, Frances, Betty, and she. The sun was setting on the final day, and there'd been no sign of life in the O'Brien house. The brown bags stood upright on their porch within the red flapping canvas. There had been the sign of death: Several people reported seeing Robert O'Brien's spirit here and there in the village. Some said he wasn't alone, that he communed with another spirit. Surely it should be his wife's but the gossip held that this other spirit was young, like Elizabeth O'Brien—though it didn't appear to be she either. Just gossip. Rumors. All of it. . . . This small band of the choir would sing in front of the O'Brien house just as night came on, praying that the rhythmic Word would rouse the family; or at least one member, who could prevent the great burning, and the village could return to normal. The church basement had its familiar musty odor, like the dust of a thousand sermons mixed with sticky furniture wax. It could be suffocating if one thought of the smell too long. Wanda was at the diminutive blue-painted desk in the corner of the basement, her desk as choir director. She heard the door open at the top of the stairs, then the heavy steps as someone began to descend. Her back to the new arrival, she tried to anticipate which choralist it was.

We say, it was summertime and that the sun coruscated like coins of silver off the ripples in Peach Creek. The crops were doing well that year. It'd been a wet spring but a persistent wind was fanning the fields dry. If it kept up, it might make them too dry—but that was the farmer's lot in life: to pray for rain, then to pray for the rain to cease; to pray for wind and warmth, then to pray for them to cease. There was always some other condition to pray for, and rarely one to be wholly thankful for. It was summertime, and the bluegill and pumpkinseeds were hungry beneath the silvery surface of the Peach.

It was nearly sundown. James Reynolds pulled on his sweater and left his house. He hoped it would be a cool evening. He walked up Parker Street to Willow. Overhead, leaves trembled in the trees, like they too were anxious and afraid. He heard the choir before reaching Willow—their raised voices blended with the maiden's whispering in his ear—all that plus the wind in the trees, and his thoughts were as chaotic as the weeping leaves and lashing branches. A crowd had already gathered. There were lanterns here and there, yet it was difficult to recognize everyone immediately. There was Mayor Bishop, standing with Mr. Holcomb and Dr. Halverson. A group of women stood apart: among them Mrs. Anthony, Mrs. Olstetter, and Mrs. Wilson. The skirts of their dresses whipped in time with the canvas portal. Pastor Anthony didn't add his voice but he stood near the five singers led by Mrs. Holcomb. Mr. Wilson was there, with Mr. Owens and Mr. Goodpath. Off to the side, more alone than anyone, was Mr. Oliver. Lantern shadows flickered across their faces, casting them as much in darkness as in light. How are you doing, James? At first he believed it was the dead maiden touching the question to his ear, then he sensed Margaret Olstetter's presence near him on the walk. I'm all right. Perhaps the wind had slowed, but the canvas on the O'Briens' porch flapped noisily. In the street, Mr. Jones and his volunteers waited near their equipment. The Merriweather's brazen body glinted in the lanternlight. James noticed that Mr. Oliver was moving his lips as if quietly reciting. James listened to the maiden's words and began repeating the words aloud, barely audible, but Margaret noticed. A light suddenly shone in the O'Brien house—a bright flame in the house's blackness. A gasp ran through the crowd. Some of the singers stopped singing. Mr. Oliver stopped reciting. James did not. The candleflame moved away from the window. The remaining choralists' voices faltered further in the darkness as the light disappeared into the interior of the house. James felt Margaret's hand slip inside his. He hadn't ceased his own whispering recitation. The dead maiden's lips touched his ear still, though even they may have begun to tremble.

Sheol

Sheol

You know quite well, deep within you,
there is only a single magic
—Hermann Hesse

The weight of the year rested heavily upon him. It had turned him into a sort of mascot for the village. There was talk of his coming birthday, his one-hundredth, in Owens' Café, in Reynolds' barbershop, in the post office. Mrs. Heartwood had made a special display at the library: The Ralph E. Stevenson Century—various pictures of him tacked to the bulletin board, a timeline from 1857 to 1957 with colored yarn stretching to hand-printed slips of paper, each noting a significant event that happened in his lifetime from Antietam to the Archduke's assassination to the atom bomb, and mixed in between milestones of his own: his school matriculation, his wedding day, the births of his daughters, Clara's death, and so on. Mrs. Davis, the upper-grades history teacher, was having her students do a report on one of the national or world events. Mrs. Wilson, the English teacher, was having them write a poem about him. The three best poems would be recited by their young authors at a celebration in his honor.

Old Man Stevenson experienced none of the hullabaloo firsthand. Bitty Fergusson reported to him about the goings-on when she visited the farm each day to cook and clean. She had been coming there for nearly thirty years, since she'd graduated from school, number-two in her class of four. She was the only person who called him Ralph. To everyone else he was Old Man Stevenson, a name he'd first heard when he was fifty. He'd been *Old Man Stevenson* and the farm had been *Old Man Stevenson's place* for half a century.

He sat in a rocking chair on the screened-in porch watching the corn move in windblown waves. The stalks were brittle and harvest brown. He'd ceased his own harvesting when he was seventy or seventy-one, and hired it done. He missed the sense of completion, the joy of it, sitting in the seat of the Minne-Moline, pulling the wide combine and its receiving bin while fields picked clean fell astern in a rush of stubble, dust and strips of papery husk rising into the sweetly pungent air.

For a moment he was riding the tractor again, the seat jogging rhythmically with the rise and fall of the furrows, but realized the sensation was simply the rocking of his chair on uneven boards, propped in the seat by too many cushions. They made the chair less comfortable but without them the seat was too low and he couldn't push himself to a standing position, the rheumatism in his shoulders and hips was too severe.

When he could no longer operate the harvesting equipment, he cultivated a long rectangle in his backyard for a vegetable garden—it helped to scratch his itch to grow—but over time the garden had to be scaled back and ryegrass sown as the garden plot retreated. *Retreated* was a good word, for that was how it felt: defeated by Time and on a slow, futile retreat from Death. At least, he thought, I have my mind enough to know my state. Clara, my love, you lost your faculties too young and died among strangers in my arms. . . .

His reverie was interrupted by a crow, the largest he could remember, landing on the shoulder of the tattered scarecrow in what remained of his garden. It fanned its wings once as it settled its taloned toes on the wood beneath the scarecrow's faded flannel shirt.

Shoo! he said . . . or thought he'd said, then realized the word hadn't left his tongue, stuck there like a stubborn postage stamp. He was too far away for the command to matter anyway.

The crow angled its head so that one eye seemed to stare at him.

Shoo! This time the word came out but only as a dull whisper.

The crow issued a chilling caw before turning and plucking a button-eye from the scarecrow's burlap face then flying off with the button grasped in its ebon beak. He followed its flight and soon the bird became a black smudge in the clouds.

Here you are, said Bitty Fergusson. I'm sorry, Ralph—didn't mean to give you a start, thought you must've heard me banging around in the kitchen.

He'd only heard his thudding pulse. It's all right, he managed, his gaze still fixed on a black speck that may have been the crow, or just a floating mote in his eye.

I put the coffee on, bring you a cup in a minute.

He watched for the crow to return for much of the morning, until he was forced to relieve his bladder. More than once he thought he saw the black thing descending, swooping down, but it was just a dark place in the clouds that dissolved to nothing after a moment or two.

Do you know which suit you're wearing to the party? They were in the farmhouse's kitchen, and Bitty was snapping beans for his supper, his only full meal of the day. At night he would have some cheese and crackers and a can of beer.

Suit, he repeated.

Yes, for Friday—for your birthday party.

He'd all but forgotten. The village was celebrating his birthday at the harvest festival.

The gray one or the navy blue? Bitty tried again.

He thought for a moment. He saw again the crow plucking out the button-eye. The black one, I'll wear the black one.

Bitty stopped snapping. Your black suit. Thought you were saving that one.

I have been. He pawed the newspaper off the kitchen counter with arthritic fingers to return to the porch and wait for his supper. And don't think I'll forget which suit I want and try to slip the blue one past me, Bitty Fergusson. I'll remember.

II

He often dreamed of Clara. They were half-waking dreams which he could partly control with his conscious mind. It was always Clara of about thirty, the Clara of about their tenth year as man and wife. They'd been finished with having babies for a while—Doc had warned them after nearly losing the last one, and Clara too. It took a long time but Clara had recovered her health. She wasn't the wispy girl she'd been when they married. His grandfather, also Old Man Stevenson, used to say that a strong westwind would lift her right up and blow her all the way to Crawford. But at thirty she'd filled out, finally had meat on her bones, and was beautiful, like a mystery woman who'd come to the county fair from somewhere distant and a bit dangerous, all the way from St. Louis or Indianapolis or even Chicago. He hadn't realized Clara's transformation until one day returning from the south field for supper he saw her from a distance hanging laundry on the line. He didn't recognize her for a long moment, the bewitching stranger in Clara's favorite housedress, the white one with the purple flowers, her chestnut hair blowing in her eyes, a clothespin in her mouth. He'd been shy around her for a few days after that, especially in the bedroom, until he became accustomed to the fact this beautiful woman was his wife, the mother of his daughters. She perhaps wondered at his shyness, which may have seemed like coolness to her—but there would've been too many chores, too many demands on her time to wonder for long.

The dreams of Clara had become more and more vivid over the years. Some nights they were more real than what he knew to be reality, which took on the air of a theater set, as if every wall of every room was painted plywood, every object a cheap prop. Perhaps that was why he selected the black suit for the birthday celebration: it seemed the most appropriate costume.

On this night he dreamed of Clara standing in the garden where the scarecrow now stands. She appears as rigid as the scarecrow, her arms outstretched as if for an embrace, and her gaze as expressionless as the dummy's, her brown eyes as dull as buttons. He can see the crow coming from the fathomless distance behind Clara. Just a black line upon the sky, like a child's drawing of a blackbird, but it soon takes form and every feather, each talon spur, the curve of its pointed black beak—all are well-defined as the enormous crow alights on Clara's shoulder.

He forced himself to awaken before he could witness what he knew was coming.

As he lay in the dark room, his back and shoulders sore and stiff from being in bed, he returned to the familiar subjects of mortality and the afterlife. In spite of attending church services for nearly a century, his concepts of heaven and hell were gauzy and as amorphous as creeping fog. The part about the soul's traveling to one place or the other seemed mistaken. Those places sounded too distant, and the dead seemed nearer, sometimes just barely beyond his reach. More and more Clara was that way. She occupied his thoughts so vividly, especially as he sat on the screened-in porch mesmerized by the waving fields of crops, he believed he could take hold of her if he could just will his mind to make the last few turns into Clara's after-place. He imagined it like that, like in the optometrist's office in Crawford, when the doctor would adjust the lenses in the overlarge spectacles of circles and gears—*better one, better two?*—clicking . . . clicking . . . until letters came crisply into view. That was the feeling: if he could make just another click or two, Clara would appear before him and he could put his hands upon her firm shoulders and look fixedly into her eyes, wells of brown plumbed to infinite depths.

This sense of *closeness but just beyond reach* frustrated him sometimes to the point of tears—warm, dewy tears that wetted his pillow in the dark. Such tears ran along the deep-set creases of his face on this night, but he realized there was something quite different at work—the heaviness of loss didn't lie upon his heart. Instead his heart fluttered and skipped, as if too light to stay pinned within his bony chest.

Lying awake in the dreaming darkness—the clock in his bedroom ticking loudly—he thought of the harvest festival and his birthday celebration, and it seemed to him that the event must be some sort of passage to the place where Clara was, the place that felt like neither heaven nor hell. Perhaps she had returned to the farm to escort him to the after-place, the region where she'd been since she'd passed. One-hundred was after all a special number, and special numbers had powers—the Almanac said so, and the Bible.

But what of the menacing crow?

Like all crows, it was up to no good. It was intent on blinding Clara—so that she couldn't find her way back, so that she couldn't lead him to the after-place. The pieces all fit together perfectly in his nighttime calculus; yes, his figuring was as rock-solid as a mathematical proof:

He must kill the no-good crow, or at least drive it away for good.

The crow perched between Clara and him, casting such a shadow with its enormous wingspan that it blotted out Clara completely, as if behind a heavy black curtain. Or worse, the crow was a plague that took Clara from him, making him relive the eclipsing devastation of her loss. The image of his slingshot returned to him. As a boy he'd become quite proficient with it—he recalled killing the jay that regularly raided the corncrib. He let fly the smooth stone and it caught the thieving bird in flight. The jay fell to the ground, suddenly like a stone itself, a single blue feather fluttering in the air a moment to mark the murderous impact. He remembered the joy and terror of it—the joy of having executed the shot so masterfully and the terror at having killed so efficiently and easily—the way the hand of God must also kill, and surely he was no worthier than the jay in God's esteem. Throughout his youth the thought of a sudden death from a divine hand lingered like an after taste of something tainted.

The irony now, anticipating his one-hundredth birthday, of having lived all those years with the vague fear of God's white-hot stone, blazing like a comet, suddenly smiting him: if he possessed more energy, he would pursue the anger it kindled in him.

But, no . . . he must save what remained of his strength for the ordeal with the crow.

III

It had become cold in the night and a weak, beclouded sun did little to reverse the chill. Nevertheless he'd pulled his heavy coat around himself as best he could and went to the porch. The cold settled into his legs through the dark-blue denim of his dungarees. He must watch for the crow. Propped next to his rocking chair was the Louisville Slugger baseball bat which normally rested in the umbrella-stand in the front hallway. It was there for any disreputables who showed up at the farm. It hadn't moved from its place in more than thirty years, other than for Bitty Fergusson's housekeeping. The bat was far heavier than he recalled and it took effort to lift it from the stand, making his shoulders ache, but he half dragged it and half used it for support to place it on the porch. Then he'd retrieved his old coat and went to the rocking chair for his vigil.

He wasn't sure how he'd lift the bat to swing at the crow, nor, for that matter, how he would be able to creep up on it; but trying to throw a rock or some such projectile was beyond reason, as was loading the twin-barrel Remington. He could only hope that strength would be found when needed, and that the crow would come before Bitty Fergusson arrived as she would no doubt interfere with his plans.

As he sat on the screened-in porch watching for the crow he entertained an indefinite sense that Clara would help steady and direct his aim with the bat. Perhaps that is why he dreamed of her in the garden . . . the crow sensed her too, which is why it menaced her scarecrow figure. He enjoyed the daydream of working with Clara to remove the crow's meddling. He saw himself as a much younger, fitter man—a husband more to match his beautiful wife. Again and again he imagined himself clubbing the crow from its perch on the scarecrow's shoulder—he imagined Clara's strength running fibrously through his limbs like lightning. The crow caws angrily and spreads its wings in electrified surprise as the baseball bat meets its feathered form. One black feather . . . two black feathers flutter upon the air at the bird's sudden demise.

The whole scene had etched itself in his mind's eye so deeply that it took some time for him to realize the crow truly was there in his garden, perched provokingly on the old scarecrow, with its solitary eye. He pushed himself upright from the stack of pillows in the rocker, the creaking of the floorboards seeming as noisy as breaking bowls, even to his ancient ears. He peered through the thick lenses of his eyeglasses, and the crow hadn't moved. He wrapped his bony fingers around the knob of the bat and he began his slow, creeping attack upon the nemesis bird.

The old man pushed open the screen-door, with its whining hinges. Using the bat for support, he took an unsteady sideways step down. There were only three steps but each was its own dramatic episode. At last he stood on the brick patio and turned toward the scarecrow, certain that the crow had absconded at the sound of the door's rusty hinges followed by the wooden thud of the bat's barrel on the steps. But, no, the bird stood on the scarecrow's shoulder casually preening itself, as concerned about the old man as it was the featureless cloud cover overhead.

The crow's ease aggravated him further. He was no more than twenty or so paces from the bird. The scarecrow, planted in the small plot of garden that remained, was amid the tendrilled remnants of tomato and cucumber plants. He slowly but purposefully made his way toward the fearless crow, whose weight tilted the scarecrow's shoulder a bit in spite of its solid support.

He paused leaning on the bat only a few feet from his prey, who insolently still paid him no heed. He wondered if he'd died in the night and was no more than a phantom. He looked for his shadow and found none . . . but soon discovered nothing was casting a shadow in the overcast, colorless day. He further surveyed the yard for Clara—for surely she would come if he'd passed in the night.

He determined he was still living flesh, and to reach his wife he must smash this foul bird.

He held his wheezing breath and tried to lift the bat into position for the fatal swing. Up, higher, up—his eye on the crow, which had stopped grooming itself and was just standing, dull black wings folded against its dull black sides, watching the mildly entertaining spectacle of the old man and his baseball bat. He realized the bat was little higher than his hip and ascending no farther. It would have to do.

He took a shuffling step into the unkempt garden while attempting to deliver something like a pugilist's uppercut. The barrel of the bat struck the torso of the scarecrow, making barely a sound it was wielded so impotently. The force of the impact nevertheless shocked him off balance and he fell like a paper doll into the clinging vegetation, ending supine and blinking at the perfectly white sky through glasses that rested akimbo on his face.

The crow squawked and flutter-hopped onto the scarecrow's other shoulder so that it could peer down at the old man more directly. They stared back and forth, and for a moment it seemed that the crow contemplated flapping down upon him, perhaps coming to perch on his heaving chest. Instead, the bird issued a parting caw and lifted himself into the chapeled sky.

Frustrated and embarrassed, the old man sensed his

brittle bones against the hard earth and waited for Bitty Fergusson to find him in the garden patch.

IV

A cold rain had been falling for two days. Bitty convinced him he didn't need to sit on the porch and expose himself to the damp, chill air. The argument was more easily won than perhaps she'd anticipated. He didn't want to risk a fever or cough or any sort of illness that would interfere with his plan to go away with Clara. From inside his house he glanced now and then toward the garden, and even the crow was avoiding the inclement weather.

The day dragged on like a sermon delivered by a monotone minister until finally it was time to dress for the harvest celebration. Bitty Fergusson had to help him with the buttons of his white shirt, the knot of his blue-striped tie, the ties of his black shoes, and finally into the black suit coat. Then she draped his overcoat on his hunched shoulders and led him to the passenger side of his pickup truck holding an umbrella over his head. He insisted that she drive him to the harvest celebration in his own truck—It hasn't been run in too long, he said.

The celebration was held in a war-built hanger that was never used for its intended purpose. For the festival, the village had strung colored lights along the frame of the hanger's arched roof, as well as the door and window frames. The celebration included a masquerade for those who wanted to participate. Adults and children costumed as their favorite saints, in old sheets and blankets and cast-off clothes, with makeshift props, hurried here and there through the gray mist. The mist added a halo effect to the hanger's strands of colored lights, and with the strangely garbed figures rushing into the structure, his theory seemed to be confirmed: the harvest celebration was a portal that could deliver him to Clara and their after-place.

Yet at the same time it wasn't purely magic and to some degree he would have to take matters into his own arthritic hands.

Inside the hanger he was greeted as a visiting luminary. Mrs. Heartwood had brought the bulletin board from the library, and he spent a few minutes lingering over the decades of his life while Bitty Fergusson fetched him a cup of hot cider. Looking at all the events, especially the national ones, like Edison's incandescent light and Black Tuesday, it hardly seemed possible. He recalled the county cooperative men who brought electricity to the farm. For a time he and Clara continued to light candles and oil-burning lamps at night, because they didn't trust that the electricity racing through their walls wouldn't catch the house on fire. Then in the blink of an eye everything was running on current and the old ways were discarded like a suit of clothes too far gone for mending.

He sat in an upholstered chair near the display, which rested precariously on a too-small easel. Meanwhile, well-wishers came to tell him happy birthday and marvel at his achievement, as if his long life was a science fair project he'd excelled at. He half expected a judge to pin a blue ribbon on Mrs. Heartwood's bulletin board.

Then Mayor Whittle quieted everyone so that he, on behalf of the village, could congratulate Mr. Stevenson on his inspiring longevity. Mrs. Reynolds, on behalf of the village wives, presented him with a crocheted rug to keep him warm on his beloved porch. Mrs. Wilson, the English teacher, introduced the students who'd written the three best poems about Mr. Stevenson's century. And the teenagers read their poems in unsure voices too quiet for him to make out more than a word or two now and again. The villagers sang him Happy Birthday, led by Mrs. Henderson, the church's choir director, then cake and punch were served.

Photographs were taken throughout, and the continually flashing bulbs dazzled his eyes. By the time the cake was cut, the crowd, with the masqueraders mixed in, appeared an odd and unfamiliar assembly—the saints smiled at him, sometimes covered in blood from gouged out eyes and dramatic stigmata, and sometimes with bodies wracked by torture. His mind was too full of thoughts of Clara to concentrate on the festivities. He was anxious for the focus on him to fade so that he could put his plan into motion.

Shortly after cake, a quintet of guitars, violin, snare drum and standup bass began its lively tunes. Bitty Fergusson had been attentive but eventually wandered into gossiping with the village wives, the toe of her practical black shoe tapping to the music. Bitty had been good and loyal to him for thirty years, more so than his own children and grandchildren, all of whom found lives away from the village, in some cases far away. He'd revised his will more than a decade before to recognize Bitty's devotion. He smiled to think of her surprise at his generosity. Neither of them had spoken of his will, and he'd never had any sense that her attachment to him was in hopes of being remembered in that way. He realized he would miss Bitty and her daily picking at him to eat right and take his medicine and dress warmly enough . . . and the way she looked disapprovingly over the top of her horn-rimmed glasses when he was misbehaving by neglecting his health. Bitty would be on his trail like a tracking hound the moment she realized he'd left the celebration.

But he longed to be with Clara again, and it was time. . . .

First he required assistance out of the chair. His shoulders and hips ached at the exertion and wouldn't supply the proper leverage. Fortunately a woman dressed as Saint

Seraphina, a board belted against her back, was passing by and came to his aid when he called to her. Bitty Fergusson was busy with chatting and watching the masqueraders dance a lively reel. He thought he might pretend to need the bathroom and then exit the hanger through a side door, requiring a longer walk to the pickup, but no one seemed to pay much attention to his being on the move, slow as it was, so he decided he could walk straight out the front doors. When he was outside and the cold rain pricked his face, he vaguely recalled that he'd had an overcoat when he arrived, and there may have been an umbrella too, but their absence didn't matter to him—he was so close to seeing Clara now.

Most of the vehicles parked outside the hanger were Ford trucks, and in the dark many appeared of the same unnamable color, which befuddled him at first. He opened the doors of two trucks that weren't his—he could tell immediately from their unfamiliar scents, strong with tobacco, which he hadn't used in twenty years. Meanwhile rain fell icily on his head and neck, and dampened the shoulders of his suit coat.

He located his own Ford, placed his cane across the seat and climbed awkwardly behind the wheel. Shutting the door proved especially challenging as he had to half climb out of the cab again to accomplish it. All the while, he feared being found out. Raindrops thrummed steadily on the hood of the truck. Luckily, Bitty was short of leg and had the seat moved forward, which helped him to work the pedals. Nevertheless the distance he had to depress the clutch seemed endless—but at last with clutch and brake engaged, and emergency brake released, he pushed the starter button, and the old truck rumbled to life. Another bit of luck was that he could pull forward to start his journey, so he maneuvered the gear stick on the column into first, let up the clutch, which relieved the ache in his knee and hip, gave the engine gas and began.

In a moment he was out of the village and on Highway 12 headed to his farm, a route so thoroughly imprinted in his memory that the truck seemed to know the way itself. Briefly he wondered if there were such machines now— that could drive a truck without human help—and he'd forgotten . . . No, he felt the vibration of the road and tires through his hands and arms, and the vibrating ache in his shoulders—and he sensed the truck could easily veer off the road if he lost control. He held onto the wheel as tightly as he could with his crippled fingers.

Mist appeared amorphously on both sides of the dark road, and his headlamps made them appear oddly contoured so that they seemed only partly formed granite statues, misshapen by interrupted sculptors who'd abandoned their unrealized forms. The visions combined with the black night and the reflecting light off the wet road to effect an otherworldly scene, complementing his notion that he was on a pilgrimage to meet Clara and go off with her to another sort of place altogether.

After a time the pain in his shoulders and hands subsided to numbness, and he could feel himself relaxing somewhat behind the wheel. His plan would work after all, and he reasoned that the pain had left his shoulders and hands because it had become the pain he felt in his soul—not his heart, not coronary pain—but the pain of longing for his lovely wife. He had packed the pain away to some part of himself where its sharpness was dulled. Now, so close to reuniting with her, the hurt was brought out in all its diamond-edged potency—and only one thing would dull it now: embracing her as he had for fifty-four years, her body against his, smothering and extinguishing the pain forever.

He clutched, pulled the gearshift into third and accelerated along the two-lane, which seemed to be abandoned except for his truck. Here and there the fog drifted across the road, obscuring his view for a second or two before he drove through the gray veil, which appeared solid figures. He had to trust in the knowledge that they were mere mist.

Squinting his ancient eyes and peering through his old steel-framed glasses, the foggy forms in his path appeared all manner of unlikely things: a bear reared up on its hind legs, an enormous sow on her side as if ready for suckling, a young elephant raising his serpentine trunk. . . . He and his truck passed right through these wonders. Each time, he emerged on the other side of the airy apparition with the road illuminated in his headlamps and that much closer to the farm and Clara. His heart fluttered as he concentrated on breathing evenly. He fought against a feeling of lightheadedness.

He'd forgotten about the radio. Some old-time music, filled with saints and sinners, might be just the thing to calm him. With luck, the Grand Ole Opry would be on when he turned the knob. He took his eyes from the road for a brief moment—and when he looked up again the misty figure that appeared was a woman, her hands held before her as if imploring him to stop.

He tried to brake but the truck barreled through her and the tires thumped over something in the road. He brought the truck to a stop as quickly as he could, his heart racing and skipping beats, his pulse thundering in his ears. The sound of fiddles and a banjo filled the night, making him think for a moment it was the musicians at the harvest festival, that somehow he could still hear the quintet, but soon understood that it was the radio's music.

He focused on catching his breath and calming his heart. He squinted into the side mirror. Mist drifted across the road, but otherwise it was too dark to see. He was conflicted and agitated nearly to the point of panic. He wanted to reach the farm and meet Clara—but yet the figure in the road seemed to be a woman, *what if it were Clara?* He recalled running over something in the road, *or was it his overwrought imagination and confused faculties?*

There was only one thing to do. He clutched and worked the gears into reverse. Then he began a laborious forward-and-backward movement, only a foot or two at a time, until the truck was turned around and pointing toward the way he'd come.

His headlamps shone on something in the road.

He inched the truck forward, careful not to kill the engine. His legs trembled with the exertion. Raindrops fell on the windshield as he strained to see between the wiper blades. The form lying in the road was mostly still but there seemed to be some movement. The same panic-laden question persisted, *what if I killed Clara?*, even though at some level his mind insisted that it was nonsensical.

He put the truck in neutral and depressed the emergency brake. He opened the door and stepped down to the road, which felt strange through the soles of his Sunday shoes. Cold drops fell upon his head and neck. He steadied himself against the truck, its hood warm against his hand.

The truck's illuminating beams were quickly diminished in the rainy night, so whatever lay in the road was still mostly obscured. Thoughts and images scatter-shot through his mind, and he tried to hold onto random bits of the chaos. Raindrops streaked his eyeglasses, further mystifying the form in the road.

He began walking unsteadily in the headlamp beams. After a few shuffling steps he recalled that he used a cane and that it was in the cab of the truck. No matter . . . he continued forward.

Whatever lay in the road was definitely moving, and

there were dark red patches on the road's uneven surface made by the truck's tires running over it. Amid all the confused thoughts, that deduction was clear. He felt cold rainwater soaking through the padded shoulders of his suit coat.

He took another step and bent toward the mystery, squinting through his blurred lenses, and the form took shape: it was the carcass of a whitetail deer, its broken hind legs splayed at odd angles from its broken body.

What was moving?

Still a few paces from the deer, he strained his eyes further. Icy water ran along the deep lines of his face.

Something as black as death perched on the deer's lifeless body . . .

The thing turned to him and released its curdling *caw!*

It was the carrion-feasting crow, feasting as much on the animal's death as on its dead meat.

The shock of the crow's greeting fissured through him— he reached back to steady himself with his cane, and for a long instant he remembered that the cane was in the truck. He waited, breathless, for the impact of the road, for God to finally smite him . . . when he felt a hand slip into his, steadying him. The hand was warm and gentle in spite of the calluses of a farm wife.

Clara.

Her name was sweet as clover on his lips, just as the oncoming lights blazed out of the mist like twin comets in the black night.

The Ancient World

The Ancient World

It is not even the past
—William Faulkner

R andall heard the voices crying out, children's voices. They were part of his dream world—the voices began there—but at some point he realized he was awake and he heard them still. His wife Becky lay next to him in bed gently snoring, undisturbed by the calling children. His house was absent children, his two boys grown and moved to Crawford after the service. They had not lived at home for a decade.

Randall rose from the bed. He didn't bother with his slippers, and the wooden floor was cold. He walked stiffly to a window, which was open a crack, and peered down toward the dark street. Nothing in particular could be seen in the weak light of a crescent moon. The voices however were definite—though there were too many, one atop the other, to make out the words and their meaning. The faintly acrid scent of burned leaves was carried on the cool air.

He looked back at Becky. How could she sleep through this strange caterwauling?

He must be dreaming. He peered again at the dark street and waited to awaken . . . after a few moments he had to accept that the voices were real.

Becky, still snoring, moved in her sleep.

Randall found his clothes in the bedroom and changed out of his pajamas. He left the room and made his way downstairs as quietly as he was able. His stirring woke their terrier, Archie, who insisted on accompanying his master when it was obvious that Randall was going for a walk, so he clipped the leash to Archie's collar, and they slipped out the back door.

It was a pleasant October night with a breeze that stirred leaves along the street. Archie watched leaves as if they might be an animal to chase.

The children's voices were no louder nor more distinct outdoors. In fact, the breeze and the rustling leaves interfered with Randall's hearing them. They may have been louder to the east, toward Hollis Woods, so he began walking Archie in that direction. Randall had pulled on the old sweater he kept on a peg next to the back door. He used one hand to button it up as they walked along Maple Street.

The light of the slim moon was weak but Randall knew the village's streets as well as anyone. He'd grown up here, and returned here after the service. He'd injured his hip in training and got no further from home than Fort Sheridan. Yet those few weeks in the army had given him a lifetime of stories to embellish.

Randall and Archie turned onto Willow Street, and the little terrier began growling at something in the dark. Randall assumed there was a rabbit or two about—

Then a voice said, I believe that's Archie, which means Randy must be there also. A figure came close to them on the walk, the bricks of which were uneven underfoot. Archie continued to growl. Archie Houndstooth, don't you recognize your old buddy?

Pastor Phillips? I'm sorry, we didn't recognize you.

Think nothing of it. It's nearly as black as sackcloth to-night. Archie licked the fingers of the hand that Wendell Phillips offered him. The terrier's silvery coat was high-lighted by the pale moonlight.

They stood in silence for a time, and the children's voic-es were still pitched upon the night breeze, their meaning no more clear.

What brings you out in the middle of the night, Pastor?

I . . . I had difficulty sleeping—perhaps too long of an afternoon nap. He may have smiled.

Randall hesitated. Is anything the matter?

Well . . . no—the dark figure of Pastor Phillips fidget-ed—not precisely. . . .

Randall hesitated: You're hearing them too, aren't you? The children's voices.

Yes. I woke hearing them. I thought at first I was just dreaming.

They move around on the wind but seem to be coming from the east. . . .

From Hollis Woods.

Yes. Archie was nibbling at some grass in widow Es-pejo's yard. Randall tugged on his leash, and the three of them began walking toward the voices.

Randall thought it should be a relief that someone else heard them but the pastor's involvement conferred more weight on the voices and added to Randall's unease. Archie sniffed with his nose close to the damp grass like a blood-hound.

It makes me think of the old legend, said the pastor, whose voice startled Randall. You know the one.

Hephaestus Hollis and his children. He was one of the founders of the village. Hephaestus was a widower with five children to raise. The story said that the youngest Hollis, a girl, went into the woods looking for the fairies that lived there, according to an older story still. When she didn't return, one of her siblings went into the woods looking for her, then eventually another for both of them, then another and so on. Hephaestus and his neighbors searched for the children for days but no trace was found. Some gossiped that Hephaestus, a simple leather-worker, had too many mouths to feed and was responsible for their disappearance. In any event Hephaestus married a widow in Crawford with two children and her dead husband's profitable dry-goods store. Villagers liked to tell the tale to their children on autumn nights, like this one, gathered around a campfire.

Randall hadn't been thinking of it when Pastor Phillips reminded him. With the recollection came a thin marbling of trepidation—and with that an irritation toward the pastor. Why was he referencing a legend and giving into superstition? Shouldn't he be attributing the voices to angels, perhaps come to deliver a message from God? Randall glanced over at Pastor Phillips. Who's to say it was Pastor at all, gliding along silent as shadow on the walk? But rather a demon sent to lead Randall to his Judgment. He had lusted after all—the new girl in town, the one who calls herself Frankie. She was in a green dress at church. It was appropriate, yet clung to her in a way that accented the lines of her adolescent body. He had thoughts of her the likes of which he hadn't had in years—sitting right there in the pew, next to his wife, watching Frankie above his hymnal as she went to the altar for the children's blessing and returned along the side aisle, hands clasped before her. Randall imagined her hands clasped that way but around him as she stared shamelessly into his eyes. . . .

Yes he very well may be punished for those thoughts. He should be. He looked again at Pastor Phillips's form. Shouldn't Archie be growling and barking if it was a demon sent to do him harm?

The trio turned onto Main Street and walked past the village square with its gazebo, which, painted white, glowed wanly in the dark.

The children's voices grew louder and distinct enough that Randall now sensed that they were perhaps not children after all, not strictly speaking, but rather girls, adolescent girls. What were they saying, the several voices laid one atop another? The wind seemed to be rising just as the voices were becoming more distinct so that their meanings remained obscure.

Randall's mouth and throat were dry. He feared the voices called out to him and soon everyone would know of his lust. He desperately wanted to hear them clearly. He thought of one of the Greek stories he learned in school, about the furious women who visited terrible punishment on men for their misdeeds. He imagined the girls like those terrible women, perched in the trees of the pitch-black woods. Angry and wrathful.

His heart fluttered against his breastbone and he wished that he'd taken Doc Higgins's advice to reduce his weight. He realized it was now Archie leading him, the little terrier pulling the leash taut and beckoning his master forward. Randall loosened his sweater and undid another button of his shirt to try to get more air.

They were nearing the corner at Division Street, which led to an entrance into the woods, when they encountered another person out walking. It was only a dark form in the still darker night, and it didn't ease Randall's anxiety.

They all converged at the corner.

Hello, said the form in a familiar voice. Who is it?

Doc? said Pastor Phillips.

Pastor?

Yes, and Randy.

And Archie, said Doc as the terrier shook his ears and rattled the metal tags on his collar.

They were all silent for a moment.

Then Doc said, What do you think they're saying, the voices?

Randall's mouth was too dry to speak, his tongue like sandpaper against his hard palate. It kept him from lying, from bearing false witness, for he heard them now—plain upon the operatic wind: They called out his lust and his covetousness. The adultery in his heart rang out in the night as clear as cracking ice. Shards of that splintered ice pierced his pounding heart as his knees buckled.

Archie strained at the leash, his senses exploding with distantly recalled images. He pulled hard at the restraint until it became difficult to breathe. Still, the images beckoned him more and more urgently. He pulled in spite of his vision beginning to grow dim. Yet his faltering vision somehow allowed him to sense the beckoning images with greater clarity.

Then the restraint was absent and he bounded into the ancient place. In a moment all of his senses merged into a single vibrant tableau, as if his sensory mechanism was a sphere that surrounded him and his immediate world. He extended the realm of the all-perceiving sphere up, out. The One lay upon the ground while lesser ones saw to him. But it was to do no good. The past, the present and the future stretched as a continuous thing along the skin of the sphere, and the One's life was already going to be gone. Sense-of-loss would wait. There were more pressing matters: *presences* here and there, calling out, reeking of fear. He closed upon a single caprine figure, which bolted deeper into the ancient place. He was close upon its cloven path. The farther he entered, the more finely woven became the sensory mesh of his sphere, which expanded in all directions like a flowerhead greeting the dawn in supplicant prayer. The fine mesh brought forward, as if from a clearing mist, little ones, five in all, clinging together in their own veil of fear, cold to their cores. The caprine runner and he crashed through the ancient world, while, above, corvine shadows perched in the black trees—but hunted and hunter could not resist the call that sounded through their blood—a deafening vibration to persist to the very edge of the ever-expanding perception.

Bitterness on the Tongue

Bitterness on the Tongue

There is a whole in the world
—Edna St. Vincent Millay

More coffee, Doc? His eyes continued to dart toward the bedroom door, waiting for it to open, hoping that it would, hoping that it would not.

Doc Higgins held the ceramic cup in both hands. It was cool to the touch and the coffee it held seemed even colder than the room itself, and it had baked to the color of tar. Yes, Jim—thanks, just a splash.

Taking the cup to the kitchen and pouring more of the terrible coffee would afford Jim Heartwood a break from watching the bedroom door, perhaps even from thinking for a moment or two about Barbara and the baby. All right: about Barbara. The baby was beyond thought, beyond worry, already becoming grief. And grief wasn't a thought. Grief was a place . . . a place where one lived—in Grief— perhaps forevermore. Thanks, Jim.

Jim's overalls were draped across his frame as if upon a scarecrow in his field. In fact his body seemed like old wood nailed together, moving cracked and splintered beneath his loose clothes as he creaked across the livingroom into the kitchen to put more of the hours-old coffee in

Doc's cup. Doc half expected a murder of crows to alight blackflapping on the furniture at Jim's departure.

In a moment Jim returned. Doc took the cup with another thank-you, and there was nothing more he could think to say. It felt like the word-making part of his brain was utterly exhausted. Jim meanwhile arranged his wooden bones into a chair that was too small for his scarecrow frame and his arms angled wearily, looking like broken wings.

Doc brought the bitter coffee to his lips and moistened them. He hoped the smell of scorched coffee would enliven him so that he could speak—any words, leave be ones of wisdom or comfort.

With relief he heard the earliest birdsong begin in the predawn blackness. The long terrible night was nearly over. Time was inching onward, and it alone could accomplish what was beyond his science and his art.

A cooling breeze entered through the screens, pulled in from the night by a box fan in the kitchen window, but with the arrival of morning summer's oppression would return, seeming full on by eight o'clock. The birds would cease their singing for the duration of the long hot day.

Doc moistened his lips again with the brew, as bitter as wormwood.

Jim bolted standing as if anticipating the opening of the bedroom door a moment before it actually did. It swung out slowly and Sarah Goodpath, the midwife, stepped into the hall. She was carrying a wash basin of liquid (bloody water, Doc imagined). Sarah closed the door with her shoulder and foot. The starch was fading from her dress, which was sycamore-bark brown, as dark as her tightly fixed hair, though a few filaments of white had come unpinned.

Doc had never seen her looking so weary. He knew

that in part she was weary from prayer—a great internal weariness from trying to bend God's will. Doc, who'd been the village's physician for more than thirty years, well understood weariness of that sort. He'd been wanting to call Pastor Phillips for a few hours but Barbara wouldn't hear of it and Jim was in no state to override her. Nor was Doc.

Sarah, still by the closed door, shook her head.

Is she holding out hope? Doc realized his hands were trembling and he tried to steady them.

I don't believe it's so much holding out hope, Sarah said quietly, then blew a strand of hair from her ashen face.

What then?

Sarah stepped away from the door and looked at Jim, who had sat again and was balanced unsteadily on the edge of his small chair. I don't know if she understands about the child. She talks to it, coos to it—like you would.

She must be in shock. Doc placed his cup on an end table—there was a picture of Jim and Barbara in a yellow frame, likely their engagement portrait. They probably believed then that the house would soon be overrun with little ones. Their radiant faces showed no hint of the years of waiting, of the years' effects.

There are cases, right? said Jim, wavering on his chair's edge as if blown by a breeze. It's happened before, and not just in the Book . . . isn't that right, Doc?

Well, I suppose, Jim—yes, there are cases . . . but they're extremely rare.

So it's possible . . . maybe Barbie knows something you and Sarah don't—a mother's intuition, something like that.

Doc and Sarah looked to each other. Her exhausted eyes, exhausted to a depth not possible within the skull, seemed to warn Doc against giving false hope, warn against a weight that would crush Jim Heartwood.

Well, I suppose, Jim.

Sarah . . . would you come here?

Sarah lowered her eyes and reentered the bedroom, still holding the basin she'd meant to empty. The door clicked shut—a sound that separated two very different worlds. A scent escaped the room, something both antiseptic and sweet, like iodine and lilac.

Doc scratched his ear and looked at Jim, who now seemed his adversary in a way. They occupied different truths, and somehow Barbara must find her way to Doc and Sarah's truth. He'd been counting on Jim to be her guide but now that wasn't possible. He thought of the ancient Greeks' ferryman transporting souls from the realm of the living to the realm of the dead. An imperfect metaphor yet the image lingered.

So much so that when Doc heard a scraping sound of wood on wood, he at first heard it as the ferryman's pole against the side of his shadowed bark, a sounding from the depths of Doc's dreaming imagination. He snapped alert as he realized it was Jim's chair legs upon the oaken floor.

I need to check the garden, make sure the rabbits haven't burrowed beneath the wire in the night.

Doc looked out the front screendoor, and the first eastern streaks purpled the pieces of sky that could be seen in the Heartwoods' tree-filled yard. The leafy trees were lavender-black silhouettes against the lilac canvas. He thought of exiting through the screendoor too, of simply walking out of this hard place—he would feel as a man struggling in a river when he pulls himself into the safety of a boat, his anxiety instantly a thing of history, of memory only. But Doc felt a vague yet potent sense of obligation to remain. Watching the lavender sky bleed to palest blue, a *fragile blue*, he'd heard it called once in a poem, Doc sorted through each member of this confined universe—Jim, Barbara, Sarah . . .—and it became clear that his duty-bound feeling rested with the child. Doc was there in the Heartwoods' home to tend to mother and child if need be, and tending to Barbara was beyond him. There was still service his oath owed the child.

Doc stood and walked past the bedroom with Barbara, Sarah and the child to the small room that the Heartwoods had prepared as a nursery. It was dimly lit by the still fragile daylight, which lent a semi-stability to the items in the sparsely furnished room, as if they had been nearly realized but were now fading back from whence they came. There was a small bureau with an attached mirror (Doc glanced at his unshaven, haggard reflection, still half in night's shadow), a hamper, a corner cabinet, and of course the crib, painted white with stenciled star-shapes, stars that wore tails like comets. They were unordered, chaotic. Beneath the window was a child-size desk and chair, both simple and unadorned, probably pine (Randall Houndstooth, the furniture-maker, could fashion such a set of a weekend). Upon the desk were two stacks of books, children's books no doubt. Doc, suddenly bone tired, went to the little desk, pulled out the chair, which felt of solid construction, and he squatted on its low seat.

Barbara was the village's librarian and had ways of acquiring even the rarest books. These were clothbound, except for one or two in leather. They seemed old, of the previous century, and not from any library's collection. These books belonged to the Heartwoods.

Doc opened one gilt-edged volume, a translation of Slavic folktales, and turned to a story titled *The Tailor's Lost Son*. There was a haunting illustration at the beginning: a child with overlarge forlorn eyes peering from an oval, ornately framed mirror. The child is wan, its hair hanging unevenly, and beyond the gaunt child the reflected room is dim and sparse, as hopeless as the child's expression. Doc angled the book's page to catch the gradually dawning light from the window before him.

The story begins with the tailor taking his young son with him to deliver a new tunic to the viscount. He wants to impress the boy that among his customers is a wealthy and powerful man like the viscount, whose special order has put the tailor behind schedule. To save time he decides to take the shortcut through the woods, even though they can be dangerous. In fact, several villagers have been lost without explanation in the ancient forest . . .

Doc sensed someone behind him in the small room but dismissed it as his imagination.

. . . At first the walk in the woods is quite pleasant. Birds are singing and even though it is autumn there are still colorful flowers peeping out here and there along the forest path. Presently the path forks, which the tailor does not recall, nor of course which is the correct way to the viscount's castle. As far as one can see both paths are quickly swallowed in gloom. The son looks to his father expecting him to know the way . . .

Again Doc sensed someone behind him. This time he turned. He was surprised by a girl standing just inside the doorway, watching him. Sarah Goodpath had a teenage daughter, Ruth, and at first Doc assumed it was she, standing quietly in the nursery's semi-gloom, but Ruth was dark and this girl was light; Ruth had the sturdy broadness of Ronnie Goodpath, but this girl was lithe like a willow.

Hello, said Doc.

The girl wore a dark dress that contrasted with her blond hair and pale features. She watched Doc intently but did not respond to him. In fact she was motionless, except, Doc noticed, her long fingers moved at her sides, pressing the air. Perhaps the girl was a relative of the Heartwoods, visiting to help with—

I didn't go to a foster home, she said, her sudden voice surprising Doc again.

A foster home . . .

I didn't go.

To a foster home.

I never left the house.

All right.

The girl, still pressing the air with her fingers, shifted her gaze. Which one are you reading?

Doc had forgotten he was still holding the book.

Which story?

The Tailor's Lost Son.

That's a good one. But sad.

The father and son have just come to the fork in the path in the forest.

The girl stopped moving her fingers. I have to go.

Go where? Are you visiting the Heartwoods?

The girl turned to leave but stopped and looked back at Doc. It's a hard thing, a hard, hard thing, but there's no help for it.

The room had grown light enough that Doc could see the girl had green eyes, eyes as green as McCall's field in summer. You're right—there's no help for it.

The girl stepped lightly out of the nursery. Her blond ponytail was tied with a ribbon of black lace.

Doc closed the book and replaced it to the stack. The yard was becoming lighter and Jim was crossing it with his hands held before him like a penitent's. In them he carried blackberries or blueberries, an offering for his wife's breakfast, but small recompense for what Doc must take from her, from them both.

Doc heard the screendoor open and close, then he rose stiffly from the child's chair and left the nursery. Perhaps a trace of the strange girl's lilac scent lingered near the doorway. It was pleasant, and contrasted with the coffee's bitterness that lingered on his tongue.

Planes

Planes

Every love story is a ghost story
—David Foster Wallace

Bob Abernathy didn't believe in ghosts, generally, even though the Bible discusses them, but someone lived in the shadowed corner of his basement. He read the word *visitant* once and that's how he thought of him. Yes, a man, a young man, at least half Bob's age, now. The visitant had been there since Bob and Marilyn bought the place, more than twenty years before, in '31—the year of the three blizzards, and the locusts in summer, and the Pruets' grain-bin fire. Bob and Marilyn moved in, and there he was in the corner, in heavy shadow, hidden and quiet. In fact, he'd never moved or made a noise in all these years. Bob hadn't spoken of him to Marilyn, to anyone. When Bob was in the basement, for example helping Marilyn tidy up after her beauty salon customers had left of an evening, he'd sense the visitant's presence, just standing, watching, in the corner where neither sunlight nor electric light could reach.

After a time the visitant had become a comfort.

Bob had a work area in the basement with a sturdy table, a high stool with a padded seat and back support, and on two walls pegboards crowded with tools. He wasn't especially handy, not like David Holcomb, who seemed the master of all odd projects, or George Dickson, the carpenter, or Randall Houndstooth, who made furniture—but Bob enjoyed tinkering in the basement (Marilyn called it puttering), which consisted largely of his listening to the radio, drinking a warm Pabst and smoking a Pall Mall or two before it was time to go upstairs and get ready for bed. He had to rise early for his job maintaining the grain bins south of the village.

As Bob would walk up the basement steps he'd notice the visitant in his dark corner, the toe tips of his boots just at the edge of shadow, almost touching the light. At the top of the stairs Bob would pull the cord turning off the basement lights. Once he'd spoken to the visitant, a simple goodnight, but there was no response, as Bob expected.

November. Daytime. Sunless and already wintercold. Bob came home from the bins to find Marilyn on the couch in the living room holding a dish towel of ice cubes to her forehead. She'd lost her balance on the basement steps.

You're lucky you didn't break your neck. You need me to get Doc over here? Bob lifted Marilyn's hand holding the towel. Her head was scraped and red, and around her eye was swollen. You're going to have a nice shiner, Mother Goose, like you've gone a round or two with the Hurricane.

No need to call Doc. I'm fine, just clumsy.

Bob thought of the visitant. What if he'd had something to do with Marilyn's fall? It was a fleeting thought. Bob replaced his wife's hand and towel to her head. Are you hurt anywhere else?

Nothing serious. My tail feathers are ruffled I'm sure—may be sitting on a soft pillow for a while.

Do you have customers today?

Jean Reynolds and Dorothy, after supper.

You should take it easy, reschedule. I could run a note over to Carl at the shop. . . .

No, I'm fine—and it's Dorothy's first time. You know that's special.

Bob stood peering down at Marilyn for a moment. He hadn't really looked at her for a long while. She'd lost weight in recent months. The blue-checked dress, one of her favorites, hung loosely about her shoulders where it'd always been snug across the chest—her best asset they'd always joked in private. Her hairstyle was still highly bee-hived, but her head of hair wasn't as thick and it required more spray to form. It seemed grayer too. In fact, her eyes appeared grayer also, no longer movie-star blue, another of her assets, this one said in public.

You sure I shouldn't call Doc? He's probably at Owens' having his tenth cup of coffee.

I'm sure, Robert. You got something in the mail, on the table. Go take a look and leave me in peace for a spell. She patted the hand that he held lank at his side.

Bob went into the kitchen and on the table was a package just smaller than a shoebox wrapped in brown paper. The return address was stamped Calumet Models & Collectibles. It'd only been a few days but he barely recalled ordering it, from an advertisement in the *Joliet Rail Gazette*.

What in the world is it? Marilyn spoke from the couch.

A model.

A model?

It sounded interesting.

You're not going to get glue all over my kitchen table are you?

Of course not. He came back into the living room. I'll put it together in the basement—Marilyn began to speak—after your goslings have been fully fluffed, Mother Goose. I'll go set it on my table. Bob was anxious to go to the basement: he wanted to see if the visitant had moved at all, had somehow contributed to Marilyn's fall, perhaps even tripped her or pushed her off balance himself. Wild notions but he couldn't help thinking them.

The basement lights were still on. Bob stepped down the stairs more cautiously than usual. He walked across the concrete floor and placed the box on his worktable. Bob shifted his view to the darkened corner . . . and there the visitant stood, quiet, staid, watchful.

Bob thought he should say something to him but held his tongue. He left the model on the table and turned off the light at the top of the stairs.

In the night Bob dreamed of a snowfield strewn with wreckage, smoking and steaming. A propeller blade stands out of the snow almost perfectly perpendicular, the oak-wood cracked in an arc at the tip but not split. Upon the white palette is a pattern of diesel lubricant, yellow, alternating with half-dollar drops of darkly scarlet blood, as if thrown there in a fury of artistic rush. There's a wing piece as large and as hinged as the engine-hood of a Model A. The snap of fire fades in and out with the solace of wind across the site, which will be capped in new snow by morning.

Bob woke before dawn, as he always did, and felt a heaviness upon him—that's how he thought of it, as if gravity had increased overnight. He was reminded of something he'd read, that scientists believed astronauts returning to Earth would be able to actually feel gravity—perhaps this is what it would be like. Marilyn lay next to him, gently snoring, her beehive angled to one side in its net. Bob sat upright, with effort. His eyesight still blurry, he stared into the dark corners of the bedroom, and it occurred to him that the visitant had come upstairs. It was foolish—the visitant had never moved from his place. It was just that his dreams unsettled him, and this peculiar sensation of heaviness.

Bob dressed in his work clothes, and was quick about his breakfast of plain oatmeal and black coffee. Marilyn normally prepared his breakfast of course but he told her to stay in bed and rest. He was hurrying because he wanted to stop by the library on his way to the bins. He maintained the ones on the northwest corner of Old Man Stevenson's fields.

Mrs. Heartwood was just unlocking the library when he stepped from his pickup and came to the door. My, you're up with the birds, she said, pulling open the door with one hand and adjusting her eyeglasses with the other. I don't think you or Marilyn have any books in. Bob liked books about history and biographies of statesmen and military leaders, while Marilyn preferred mystery novels, especially Conan Doyle and Wilkie Collins, and she also enjoyed Poe.

I'm in the market for something else, said Bob, and he went directly to the book he wanted (meanwhile, Mrs. Heartwood switched on the one-room library's lights). He'd noticed the book for years but never checked it out: *North's Illustrated Encyclopedia of World War I Aircraft*. The heaviness that he still felt seemed to slow him down but he was relieved *North's* was there on the shelf.

The grain bins were a hive of activity throughout the fall but by November the fields had been reaped, except for the winter wheat, the short green stalks of which waved against a cold and colorless sky. So the bins stood apart from the stubbled fields that stretched south and east waiting to be covered in snow and kiss completely the color-drained sky. The bins were cylinders of stone and sheet metal as tall as a tall house, with black scaffolding that rose up in support of the structure, and a conduit arm which hung down like a cripple's. Even though each bin's single arm was securely tethered with thick cable, they rocked somewhat in the persistent wind and gave the impression of animation, like large machines that have arrived from another world. The bins had names that added to the impression of animation; they were Sadie and Katie and North, who took the wind most directly and his arm moaned and winced against the tethering cables.

After checking out the book, Bob had felt that someone was following him on his way to the bins. He noticed the unfamiliar truck in the rearview mirror of his own Ford. It got close at times but there was something about the way its windshield glass reflected the colorless sky that prevented Bob from seeing the driver. Bob turned onto the side road that led to the bins, and the pickup, black with a dull gray fender, very similar to his pickup, continued down Highway 12. Still, it made him uneasy. As he pulled onto the graveled patch near the bins, he realized he thought it was the visitant behind the wheel of the strange truck. He'd never been anywhere except the dark corner of the basement, but Bob felt that he was becoming bolder, perhaps causing Marilyn to hurt herself and now this. . . .

Bob looked forward to the quiet and calm in the office, a single-story brick building with a tin chimney. He could drink a cup of coffee from the vacuum bottle which he'd packed himself and thumb through *North's Illustrated Encyclopedia*. He'd ordered several models of aircraft from the Great War, but their catalogue numbers gave no indication which airplane they were. He wanted to be able to identify them. Without their correct names the models would seem incomplete, no matter how much care he put into building them. He wanted to know what sort of engine propelled them, how fast they could fly and to what altitude, what sort of armaments they carried, and how well they maneuvered in dogfights. Knowing everything about them was important to him.

The bins required daily inspections. Bob would remove the access panels to check the drying motors, the belts and gears and diesel lines, the ignition chamber and the ductwork. Then he'd climb the scaffolding to make sure the vents were clear, that no animal had nested inside the venting hoods. The routine took longer than thirty minutes for each bin, but the thoroughness was necessary to prevent catastrophes like fires and even explosions, or mildewed grain. While he went about his business, his sense of being watched returned. It seemed there was someone at the edge of the cylindrical bin, spying, who would step back out of sight the instant Bob glanced his way; and several times, on the scaffolding, Bob peered over his shoulder at the empty fields expecting to find the visitant standing among the stubble, staring up at him, but each time there was no one. Only a chill wind met his squinting gaze.

At lunchtime Bob went home to check on Marilyn, and on Highway 12 the black pickup truck came up behind him. Again Bob strained to see in the rearview mirror who was in the driver seat but the beclouded sky moved across the truck windshield glass obscuring the interior of the cab.

An oncoming car honked at Bob, Wilson's mint-green Galaxie—Bob was crossing the center-line. He steered back, overcorrecting, and his passenger-side tires kicked up gravel and dust from the shoulder. Bob checked the mirror, and the black truck was gone, turned off, though he couldn't think where. Regardless, Bob felt relief with the truck no longer following him. He clutched and geared down to first to turn onto Main.

Marilyn wasn't resting on the couch as he'd expected. He went into the kitchen—another model had arrived and the box was on the table. Bob heard a voice, Marilyn's, coming from the basement, muffled by the closed door. At first he thought she was singing to herself, which she did sometimes, but, no, she was speaking, as if in conversation. He never knew her to talk to herself, not in nearly thirty years.

He had difficulty making out her words. It wasn't the same voice she used with clients, warm and chirpy, welcoming. Marilyn's voice was low and somber, like the voices at the visitation. When Robbie had died. Neighbors used the voice to express their condolences and reference God's mysterious working. Bob and Marilyn never mentioned Robbie, as if they'd never had a son, for two years and sixty-two days, as if the photograph in the plain wooden frame in the curio wasn't of a real child they'd held and loved.

Robbie now would be the age of the visitant, a young man, old enough to have a family of his own—old enough to die and leave a widowed wife and a fatherless boy of not quite three, not quite old enough to remember him, so that the vacant space in his memory could be filled only by anecdotes and fantasies. Myths that the boy created: a father who died bravely in battle, a father who was piloting an amazing air-machine. Robert Abernathy, captain. Not Robert Abernathy, farmer . . . husband, father, churchman, victim of pointless accident.

Bob was startled when Marilyn opened the basement door.

I didn't know you were home (startled too). I was restocking the towel cabinet.

How's your eye?

Marilyn had powdered around the eye more heavily. A bit tender but not bad. I was going to toast a cheese sandwich. Want one?

Sure.

Another model.

He'd forgotten he was holding the box and *North's Illustrated Encyclopedia*.

What book is that? It doesn't seem your normal fare. Not some stodgy biography.

I ordered several.

Books?

Models. They're arriving one by one. They may be hard to identify. I'll put it on my table.

I can call you when your sandwich is ready.

O.k.

Marilyn closed the basement door after him and listened to his heavy steps go down. She went about greasing the iron skillet and preparing the bread and cheese, then lighting a burner on the stove with a match. Even this simple operation tired her. Bob was quiet in the basement anyway, and with the rush of the burner flame and the sizzle of the sandwiches she couldn't hear him at all. He was as quiet as the haunt in the corner, the fellow who just stood there day upon day, as silent as Saint Benedict.

Marilyn knew the word *haunt* from the Negroes who worked in her daddy's fields when she was a girl, laborers who came certain times of year. The women prepared food in the backs of their old trucks, which seemed to barely run, and in the stone firepits Marilyn's daddy had around the place for just that one purpose. Marilyn liked to watch the women and hear the songs they sang while preparing their men's food. Sometimes they would stop singing and tell Marilyn stories, their white teeth and eyes flashing with mischief. They spoke of haunts who attached themselves to places and people, who watched with stone-dead eyes but never uttered a word. Marilyn wondered if the Holy Ghost was a haunt but didn't dare to ask her daddy; he wouldn't have liked her talking with the Negroes.

Marilyn hadn't thought of haunts for years, until she and Bob bought the old Keeling place and then one was in the basement, just standing in the shadowed corner, a young man mutely observing, the toes of his boots nearly touching the light that angled near him. Very soon Marilyn took comfort in the haunt's presence. She found it easier to talk to him about certain things than to Bob, who was prone to overworry. Like her spell on the stairs. It wasn't the first time she'd become dizzy in recent months. She thought of seeing Doc Higgins about the spells and the fact she just didn't feel quite herself. Her clothes fit more loosely, and there was the hair in the bathroom basin when she was doing it up in the morning, long dun-colored strands looking as dull and waxy as castoff thread. But if she saw Doc everyone in the village would know by noon, and by nightfall Pastor Phillips would be selecting passages to read at her service and the busybody wives would be selecting recipes for casseroles to bring to Bob.

She could always use some supplies from the beauty warehouse in Crawford. She could drop Bob at work, take the truck and see one of the Crawford doctors.

What if you become lightheaded while driving?

The question seemed to come from beyond her own thoughts.

Marilyn turned and looked about the small kitchen. Of course there was no one. It occurred to her it was the haunt who questioned her, though he'd never spoken before.

The smell of charring nipped her reverie. Marilyn turned off the burner and used the wooden spatula to lay the cheese sandwiches on plates. Before cutting the sandwiches, she opened the basement door to call to Bob—

but she was startled by his standing there at the top step—

Marilyn clutched at her chest with the hand that held

the knife. For Pete sake, Robert. You almost gave me a coronary.

Sorry, Mother Goose, I was already on my way up.

I didn't hear you. She cut the sandwiches and set the plates on the kitchen table.

Bob seated himself. Maybe we should have Doc check your hearing while he's at it. He smiled but his tone didn't sound joking.

Marilyn opened the icebox, removed the bottle of milk and poured two glasses. Her hands were unsteady and she had to concentrate not to spill some milk on the table. Fortunately Bob was already looking at a page in his airplane book and starting to finger his sandwich, though it was still too hot to eat. He didn't notice her trembling.

She gave him an opportunity to eat part of his sandwich. She played at reading her book while she nibbled at her crusts. It was a collection of Poe's ghost stories, and she looked at one titled "Morella," which turned out to be about a daughter that eerily resembles the mother who died giving birth to her. Meanwhile Marilyn snuck looks at Bob. She didn't so much see the man that sat adjacent to her, absently eating his sandwich, a small piece of cheese clinging to the stubble on his chin, but rather she imagined the man he would become in her absence. His face grew thinner, the beginning of jowls receding. His hair, streaked in silver, blanched completely white and grew past his collar. The sprouts of hair on his rough-knuckled hands turned white as well, while the age spots expanded and stood out more prominently. Overall there was a shrunkenness about him, like a heaviness had come upon him, stooping him, determined over time to collapse him altogether. She thought of the story of Bob's father crushed beneath a tractor when Bob was just a child, a toddler, not quite three. Marilyn hadn't thought of that for a long time. It was as if Robbie's death had eclipsed all deaths, before and after. No other loss mattered placed beside the loss of their son.

The current Bob, the for-the-time-being Bob, sat before her, one sandwich-half gone, the other being worked on. She said, I need to go to Crawford, to Standard Beauty. Can I take the truck tomorrow? Drop you at the bins?

He stopped chewing and looked up from his book.

Will that work all right?

Yeah—I'm just trying to think if I could use something from Crawford, from the hobby store. I could take the day—

You don't need to do that. I'm perfectly capable. Make a list and I can go by the hobby store too.

I . . .

What is it, Robert?

He chewed his sandwich a bit more. Nothing. That'll be fine, Mother Goose. I'll pack a lunch.

That evening Bob puttered in the basement longer than usual. Marilyn went to bed intending to read long enough that Bob would finish with his models and come upstairs. She could hear the voice of Bob's radio traveling through the ductwork, emitting from the floor register, sounding broadcast from a distant world. Marilyn became so sleepy the words on the pages of her book swam and bled together, implying an alien script. The book, with its strange language, slumped on Marilyn's bosom as her eyelids fluttered on the edge of a dream. The otherworldly voice became the minister's monotone at Robbie's service, his monotony adding to the pain that threatened to crush her. The words, intended to provide some sort of solace, only drew the grief down upon her like a heavy, blinding, suffocating hood.

Dreaming, she sees Robbie as a young man, dressed in work clothes ready for the fields. Dark diagonal bars of shadow fall across him obscuring his features. She wants him to speak, to account for his long absence, but he stands staring at her mutely, a stripe of saffron light across his empty eyes.

She woke with a start. Bob was next to the bed looking down at her. What in the world, Robert. You frightened me. He had switched off the bedside lamp, and only light from the hallway came into the room. Poorly backlit and standing there soundlessly, Marilyn thought for a moment it was the haunt, finally come up from his basement corner.

Sorry, Mother Goose. I'll get ready for bed.

Bob turned and went into the bathroom in the hall, shutting the door.

The strangeness of it all, especially the dream, clung to Marilyn—and she felt it even more palpably the next morning. Normally Bob was up before her but he lingered in bed. When she was dressing, he informed her from the pile of blankets and quilts that he didn't feel well and was staying home.

What's the matter with you?

He didn't respond. Marilyn thought he only acted at being asleep but she left him be and finished dressing for her trip to Crawford. After her breakfast of toast and coffee, she took the extra keys from the peg by the back door. It was a gray day threatening rain. Marilyn hadn't driven for more than a year and it felt strange to climb behind the wheel. When she shut the heavy door, its hinges cringing with rust, the scent was a mixture of Bob's Pall Malls and machine oil. The potent smell comforted her. Marilyn didn't want to make the trip alone but it was best. If the doctors at the clinic had bad news, this way she would have control over it—when to tell Bob, how to tell him, and how much.

What a comfort Robbie would be if he'd lived to grow

into a young man. A comfort to her and to Robert.

In a few minutes Marilyn was maneuvering the Ford onto Main Street, then onto the shortcut to Highway 12. The narrow road ran along Old Man Stevenson's property. It was a road she traveled often as a girl, riding with her daddy. It was a roundabout way to the village from their place but spring floods sometimes cut off the usual route.

The gray light played tricks on Marilyn's sense of time, and she had the impression it was the gray twilight of dusk, not dawn—that the world was growing darker, not lighter.

To the west, Marilyn spied the shapes of Robert's bins, like natural formations dark against the dark sky. Perhaps she also saw a solitary figure in the field near the bin they called North. In her mirror Marilyn noted that she wasn't alone on the obscure road: a black truck much like Robert's. Though the pickup was unfamiliar she sensed that she knew the driver, or at least would come to know him.

Before steering onto the highway Marilyn caught a final glimpse of the grain bins, and from this angle they appeared to be giant machines, giant machines aligned in military formation. The single figure in the field was now lost from view.

Season of Reaping

Season of Reaping

All such things that one holds to one's heart
have a common provenance in pain
—Cormac McCarthy

P astor Phillips left the backdoor unlocked and went to his office. He adjusted the thermostat to cut the chill. The church was rarely used on a Tuesday, except after supper, and Mrs. Overton, the organist, would appreciate that the sanctuary was already warm for choir practice.

The pastor heard the backdoor open and close then the footsteps in the hall—but was surprised when Mayor Whittle appeared in his doorway.

Frank—did Doc call you too?

The mayor was in his familiar well-worn denim overalls and flannel jacket. Gray whiskers stood out on his puffy cheeks and double chin. He smelled of rich earth and granulated fertilizer.

The office was already becoming warmer so Pastor Phillips removed the cap from his bald head; then he took a handkerchief from his pants pocket and cleaned his glasses while he and the mayor settled in waiting for Doc Higgins.

The mayor folded his jacket across his lap. Do you have any idea what this is about?

None, but it sounded important.

They heard the backdoor open and in a moment the doctor sat in the office's remaining chair, he and the mayor facing Pastor Phillips across his tidy desk.

Thanks very much for coming. The doctor's prematurely white hair was wild from being raked so vigorously with his fingers. His shirt of watchman plaid was disheveled. His wire-rims clung to the end of his nose and he did not push them into place as he had grown accustomed to looking at the world by peering above the circular lenses. The men had known each other since childhood and, while not close friends, they normally would have begun with some lighthearted banter; it was clear however that the doctor was agitated.

What's going on, Doc? asked Pastor Phillips.

We have a situation. . . . Doc Higgins began fussing with the nameplate on the pastor's desk, as if it required straightening. Three girls have come in the office in the last week—the first two in less than twelve hours of each other—and all three have the same condition. . . . He began to touch the base of the pastor's desk lamp—

For the love of Pete, said the mayor, just tell us what's going on.

They're all pregnant, but with all three of them their hymen is intact.

Their hymen, repeated Mayor Whittle—you mean they're virgins?

Yes—I've triple checked, *quadruple* checked . . . the tests and examinations are accurate and conclusive.

Pastor Phillips had not said anything so the mayor continued, Is that even possible, medically speaking I mean?

Yes, it's possible but very rare, and for three teenage girls from the same village, at essentially the same time . . . well, that's beyond rare. . . .

It's a miracle, said the pastor—right here in our village, in our congregation—we've been touched by the hand of God. The pastor's face was ruddy with joy behind his black horn-rimmed glasses.

Now hold on, said Mayor Whittle, let's not go calling something a miracle at the drop of a hat. Somebody's been touched, these three girls to be sure, but maybe not by the hand of God.

What are you saying? Doc Higgins turned more toward the mayor.

I'm just thinking out loud—what if it's mischief more than miracle?

You mean someone's sneaking around the village defying medical science?

Well, yes. . . .

Pastor Phillips spoke up: Or do you mean the devil? You think Satan has sown his seed in these three young women?

I don't think anything . . . just that we shouldn't slap the label *miracle* on it til we know what's what.

The pastor asked, How have the girls and their families reacted? I'm surprised not to have heard from at least one of them.

Well . . . I haven't precisely told them yet . . . I was trying to sort out the first case and then there was a second, which made it a whole new ballgame. I hinted it may be some virus that needs to run its course . . . I was thinking of calling the families in this afternoon, then bam! a new one this morning.

The mayor said, I don't mean to tell you your business, Doc, but I believe you better let these folks know a-sap.

Of course—but I wanted to speak to you two beforehand, to let you know . . . it'll affect more than these three young ladies and their families—

Three, that you know of, interrupted Pastor Phillips—there could be more, I'm just saying. . . .

Heaven help us then, said the mayor.

Let's not get ahead of ourselves. I'll call the girls into my office tomorrow and let them know, one at a time of course.

Meanwhile, said Mayor Whittle, this needs to be kept under our hats, just the three of us for now, outside the families I mean. Maybe, Doc, you could encourage the families to be discreet, for the time being at least. Are we agreed?

The doctor and the pastor confirmed that they were.

▲

Mrs. Whittle had fixed Frank's favorite, chicken and dumplings, but he barely touched the meal. After a few bites he apologized, took his coat off the hook by the kitchen door, and said he had a tractor with a wonky wheel he had to see to. In the equipment barn he turned on the overhead lights and breathed in the comforting scent of grain dust, nitric fertilizer, swine feed and diesel fuel, among a hundred potent others. He went to the shop table, where a variety of tools set out or hung from the peg-board on the wall. The tools—ballpeen hammer, needle-nose pliers, spirit-level, hacksaw, pipe-wrench, and so on—were more or less neatly arranged, and most were in good condition, others merely serviceable. For a few minutes he moved the tools from one spot on the table or peg-board to another, as if that was what he had come to the barn to accomplish. When the tools were all returned essentially to their starting points, Frank opened one of the table's metal drawers, dug beneath a layer of old receipts and half-read circulars, and he lifted out a mason jar. He twisted the stubborn lid with his heavily callused fingers, and the ripe scent of

|·)
Weep not for the blessing bestowed,
Secretly gifted in bedeviled night;
Call it not a curse claimed and owed.
 Listen well to the viola strings hard bowed,
 The moaning music sawed beyond sight;
 Weep not for the blessing bestowed.
Cleverly spawned to be piercingly sowed,
Better to be planted than to hard fight;
Call it not a curse claimed and owed.
 Great the joy in claiming the furrow hoed,
 By blessed beating powers of the light;
 Weep not for the blessing bestowed.
A swelling sign in a bark first rowed,
Whose cryptic course seems angle straight;
Call it not a curse claimed and owed.
 Each observer believes the tale to be known,
 And for this one can feel only hate:
Weep not for the blessing bestowed—
Call it not a curse claimed and owed.

grain alcohol filled his nostrils—it was homemade, given to him by Old Man Stevenson, his nearest neighbor at three miles due south on Stevenson Road. Frank carefully poured an ounce or two into a metal cup that remained of a long-lost vacuum thermos.

He took a sip and it was as terrible as he remembered; he took another. He could feel his sinuses start to run.

Frank opened another drawer and took out the book that lay on top, an old Bible with a well-worn cowhide cover. He did not look at that particular copy very often but it remained on top of the papers and other debris in the drawer because Frank felt it to be disrespectful to place anything else on top of the Good Book. It was the copy he had read as a boy. When he married, his new wife's family Bible became the Whittles' central copy—a large black-covered New American with gilt edges and a purple ribbon to mark one's place. After twenty-six years of marriage Frank did not recall how his boyhood Bible became the equipment-barn copy but he did look at it from time to time, when his mind was unsettled and he needed the familiar stories to cast some light on the world.

The moment he heard Doc Higgins's news, the old apple-worm began to gnaw at his gut. That is how he imagined it as a boy: a putrid green worm that ate away at his insides, feeding at his core, at his soul. He knew, even when very young, that he did not carry a parasite—that the gnawing was an idea, a feeling, which originated in this book, in Revelation.

Frank thumbed to the twelfth chapter and read of the pregnant woman and the dragon, of how the terrible seven-headed dragon pursued her, and how she gave birth to a son who was touched by divinity, and of how it was precursor to the coming of the Beast marked by 666, and the End Times. . . . As a boy every pregnant woman Frank encountered caused him fear, even though he did not believe she personally was the pregnant woman of Revelation. Eventually this fear associated with pregnancy, even with animals around the farm, subsided to a vague uneasiness, disconnected directly from Revelation.

But Doc Higgins's news, which certainly sounded Revelatory, revived Frank's deepest fears. If there were three, why not more? Other girls who had not come to Doc, who did not yet suspect anything themselves? What would be a proper number? Four, Horsemen . . . six, six-six . . . seven, headed . . . thirteen, the traitor's number among the Disciples—there were too many numbers of significance to say.

The familiar and troubling thought came to him that it was perhaps his deepseated fear of pregnancy which had somehow prevented him and his wife from conceiving—an idea that had always been too painful for him to voice. He drank hard from Old Man Stevenson's mason jar.

◄

For much of the day Wendell Phillips was in a kind of ecstasy, thinking of the Savior's divine conception to a virginal teenage girl. Somehow the news that Doc Higgins shared with him and Frank Whittle made the New Testament story seem more real than it ever had. As much as he had tried to give it texture beyond a mere fairy tale or myth—both in his own thinking and in his preaching to the congregation—he had to acknowledge now that he had failed. Though accepted as God's Truth, the stories—Sodom and Gomorrah, Noah, Daniel, Jonah, Mary and Joseph, all of them—had as much substance in his imagination as Red Riding Hood, as Hansel and Gretel, as Zeus' seduction of Leda.

But now he saw Mary with a vividness that startled him. He saw red dust between the toes of her sandaled feet, he saw tiny hands with chewed cuticles resting upon a swelling that seemed too large for her small frame, he saw worry-knitted crowsfeet around eyes still brilliant with youth. Mary and the Savior in her womb had come to life in Pastor Phillips's imagination, in his soul.

It was this vivid imagery that caused Wendell to go about his day in an ecstatic haze, intoxicated with joy. He had puttered about the church finding little tasks to perform until he exhausted the possibilities. He wanted to share his joy with others—not the news, he knew that was impossible—but still he wanted others to be enveloped in his euphoria. He went to the post office and asked Post Master Johnston about the arrival of a fictitious package that was supposedly en route; he bought a bottle of soda and pack of chewing gum at the filling station and spoke of the pleasant weather with Bobby Moreland, the teenage boy who worked there; he got a trim from Carl Reynolds, a week before his usual visit to Carl's barber chair.

It was when he decided he had no place else to go except home that his euphoric fog began to dissipate. For the first time all day he thought of Rebecca, his own teenage daughter, and the niggling question began to form in his mind: What if Rebecca were one of the virgins that Doc spoke of? Pastor Phillips's pace slowed as he made his way along Main Street, chewing gum, suddenly lost in his thoughts. He tried to recall his conversation with Doc and the mayor. Was there an odd tone in Doc's voice when he spoke of the three girls directly to him? A shift in facial expression? A nervous gesture of his hands? Pastor Phillips could not say with certainty but it seemed that perhaps Doc's mannerisms implied something toward him that was absent toward Frank.

And what of Rebecca herself? Had she not been acting peculiarly since before the school year began? Wendell

|·) |·)
Wary of Hollis Woods since childhood,
Lurking shadowed forms threatening harm;
And there once a menace found in the wood.
    Serpenteyed, honeycloaked and piously unshod,
    While wasps quiver the dark in a swarm;
    Wary of Hollis Woods since childhood.
The way taken snaking hard as two could,
Unknown the lurking malevolence of that charm;
And there once a menace found in the wood.
    A letting, mixing and swarming of the blood,
    Secret silence the only shrieking alarum;
    Wary of Hollis Woods since childhood.
Stranger in the dark, in the grass, in the weed,
Alien in head and heart, more alien in form;
And there once a menace found in the wood.
    A harmful appetite to nurture and feed,
    While inside and out rages a penetrating storm:
Wary of Hollis Woods since childhood . . .
And there once a menace found in the wood.

wanted to attribute her strangeness to being friends with the new girl in the village, Francine . . . there was something about Frankie's subtle rebelliousness that had rubbed off on Rebecca, or so he speculated. For years Rebecca had worn her straw-colored hair tightly cropped to control its curl, and she was so particular about the laundering and pressing of her clothes that she had long ago taken over that chore from her mother. Recently Rebecca had become indifferent about her appearance, like her friend Frankie, who managed to capture everyone's attention with no effort at all. But now Pastor Phillips wondered if Rebecca's stretches of aloofness, of solitary quietness, may be rooted elsewhere. Would it be any less of a miracle, of a blessing, if his own daughter were among the three virgins? His logic said no but there was no question that his joy felt fully tarnished.

▼

Pastor Phillips stood in the hall listening to the muffled voices drifting up from the church basement. The youth group was having its Wednesday evening meeting, led by the Burnsides, Randy and Julia, a young couple who had grown up in the village, and were youths in this same group. Randy played the guitar; and Julia baked treats, cupcakes, cookies, or brownies. They were good with the children and teens, especially the teens. The Burnsides often led discussions about avoiding temptation.

Wendell hovered near the door hoping to deduce tonight's topic but it remained elusive. There was an eruption of laughter . . . probably Bobby Moreland cracking wise—the young man was clever that way. He listened for Rebecca's voice and thought once or twice he heard a syllable or two but he was not sure, and, anyway, the voice carried no meaning. He did not bother to listen for Frankie's voice in the babel. The Burnsides had told him that the new girl mainly just sat there during youth group, not contributing to the discussion, not even adding her voice to the group songs. Wendell knew the look she would affect during such times, having seen it in his own home: a beatific smile beneath smoldering green eyes. Could Francine be among the special virgins? Surely not.

Doc Higgins had not called Rebecca into his office, as far as Wendell knew. It was not possible that his wife and daughter could have gone in for multiple examinations and consultations without his being aware of it . . . was it? And there would be special things in the house, special nutrients . . . of course there would be. Still, the idea of it, of his daughter being pregnant, plagued him. She could be without even realizing it herself. . . .

It was fruitless to stand in the church hallway so the pastor returned to his office and closed the door. It was unusual for him to be at the church on a Wednesday evening—Randy and Julia had a key to come and go as they pleased—but there had been a phenomenon during the service Sunday, a phenomenon that he found thrilling and terrifying and, most of all, bewildering; and he wanted to see if the youth group would bring forth the same . . . event.

It had been two weeks since Doc Higgins had shared his news and Pastor Phillips was at his pulpit reading Mark 6, planning to use the passage as an introduction to a newly written sermon he had titled 'Accepting the Miraculous into Our Everyday Lives.' As the spiritual leader of the village he felt it his duty to prepare everyone for the happening of which they would all inevitably be a part.

The congregants sat bovinely in the pews watching their pastor, truly with the blank expression of the cattle on Frank Whittle's farm. Wendell Phillips adjusted his black-rimmed glasses, straightened the knot of his necktie, glanced down at the Scripture before him, and read aloud, When he disembarked and saw the vast crowd, his heart was moved with pity for them, for they were like sheep without a shepherd. . . .

Wendell glanced up at the congregation and was startled by a strange light emanating from the pews. He thought for a second that he had neglected to turn on the sanctuary's overhead fixtures when he had arrived and someone had finally realized and flipped the switch; but he immediately dismissed the idea. The sudden glow was coming from the congregants themselves. The pastor squinted against the oncoming glare: specifically the light came from an aura cast by each of the teenage girls—white light tinged in rose or ice blue or blushing lavender, framing their lovely heads. And the radiance queerly lighted and shaded the other members of the congregation, transforming their features into light and dark masks as intricate and mysterious as the moon's cratered and peaked shadows. The weird glow backlit the girls' faces, making it difficult to identify who was who.

But neither the haloed girls nor the others seemed to be aware of their nimbuses.

The pastor had quit reading and was blinking against the harsh glare when just as suddenly the illumination ceased . . . and Wendell realized his congregants were staring at him quizzically. He issued a wan smile and recovered his place in Mark.

By the following day Wendell had begun to question whether the phenomenon had happened at all. He had come to the church on youth group night in hopes that the teenage girls would begin glowing again—he had even watched the space beneath the basement door for a sudden flare—but nothing out of the ordinary occurred.

He sat quietly in his office as the young people came up

|·) |·) |·)
Hard points in blinding bitter bright,
And no flowing Mercy to be found;
Drowning desperate in a sea of light.
    Found innocent on this sacred site,
    Holy head brightskinned, pearlcrowned;
    Hard points in blinding bitter bright.
And no help for this hard bitter fight,
Though arms and legs are poorly bound;
Drowning desperate in a sea of light.
    Desperation grown past mere lucid fright,
    With bitter voice breaking beyond the sound;
    Hard points in blinding bitter bright.
Threetongued speakers of skin in sight,
While sanguine rhythms surge and pound;
Drowning desperate in a sea of light.
    As unholy brightness ebbs into unholy night,
    And the sacred site becomes a burial mound:
Hard points in blinding bitter bright—
Drowning desperate in a sea of light.

from the basement and noisily exited the church; in a moment the Burnsides were heard tidying up and then leaving too. Pastor Phillips turned off his desk lamp and sat for a long while in the dark listening to the church's shifting and settling moans and creaks.

▶

Frank Whittle frequently dreamed about his cattle lowing in the fields, their white faces framing enormous onyx eyes, which, in his dreams, peered heavenward at stars like rock salt affixed to a night sky of purple onion skin. He lay for a long while next to his gently snoring wife believing he was dreaming . . . until finally he realized it was not just the lowing of cattle he heard.

He quietly crept out of bed, though the arrival of a twister suddenly tearing the roof from the farmhouse would have barely stirred Mrs. Whittle. In a few minutes Frank was at the kitchen door, having pulled on his overalls and mud-spotted Wolverines. As he dressed he listened to the peculiar hullabaloo outside.

The air was autumnally crisp, the sky clear—the quartermoon and stars lay against the sky like renderings of artists. Frank had the big metal flashlight he kept inside the door and he twisted its round head until a bluish beam shone upon the trampled-grass yard. He wondered at the whereabouts of his shepherd, Max, who slept in a large shingled doghouse next to the back porch. Normally Max was at his heal the moment Frank came outdoors. Perhaps there were coyotes and coydogs gathered where the property abutted Hollis Woods; their scents and shadowed scurryings would catch Max's attention. Frank moved the beam around the yard and saw the familiar objects—the beginnings of fences, the old rusted pump that had not brought up water for a generation, Mrs. Whittle's herb garden with a statuette of blue-hooded Mary standing among the thyme—everything now made slightly strange by the night.

Frank switched off the flashlight and stood stock-still: it seemed every animal on the property, except Max, was caterwauling in the unique voice of its species. The pigs, the cows, the goats, the chickens, even the ducks and geese at the pond, he imagined, and perhaps even the carp and bluegill gurgled beneath its verdant surface. Frank twisted on the flashlight as he walked toward the swine-barn.

Even before he slid back the barn door Frank Whittle knew the spectacle he would see; he heard it from outside, in spite of the pigs' high-pitched squealing. He did not switch on the overheads but rather shined the flashlight inside the large pen where the pigs, more than a hundred head, were scampering in a counterclockwise circle, all together, like human marathoners who could not break free of the starting pack. It was the pigs' instinctive method for cutting from the herd a member that was ill. When they sensed one of their number was faltering, they would begin this mad circular running until the sick pig fell out of sync and eventually collapsed on its side in the middle of the circle wheezing and waiting to be put from its misery. The healthy pigs would cease their running and move to the farthest side of the pen, leaving their fallen member isolated. On the farm it would be Frank or his hand that would remove the dying pig; in the old natural world a predator would fall upon the helpless animal and drag it off to its fate.

Frank shined his light about the pen but could not spot a pig that seemed to be struggling to keep pace. And normally the pigs would run in silence except for an occasional oinkish grunt. On this strange night their distressed squeals filled the barn, pealing off the walls and rafters.

It was an alien cacophony, as if made by exotic creatures from a far-off land.

Unsettled by it, Frank backed away and shut the barn door, a bit too quickly and it thudded against the frame.

Everywhere on the farm it was the same: the animals were agitated and calling forth in ways Frank had never heard, not in fifty years of farm life.

It was the small herd of goats that most unnerved him. He had the sense they had been waiting for him, bleating accusingly in their old-womanish voices, their ebon eyes staring at him like polished anthracite, as they stood tightly together in their pen. Their voices seemed almost to form meaning, their pink-tongued bleats a mere wrung or two beneath words. Frank stood cascading the beam from one wizened, bearded face to the next, their white features taking on a lazuline cast in the artificial light.

His pulse was already racing before he began jogging along the dirt path back toward the house. He had not moved like this in more than a decade. With the haphazard shaking, the flashlight went out but it was no matter as Frank knew every square inch of the property. Besides, some lunar- and stellarlight rained down from the heavens. He had nearly reached the yard when he realized the animals had suddenly become quiet again. He stood on the path leading to the goat pen and beyond that the pond, and he listened keenly to the normal silence, which now took on a lavender shade of strangeness.

The wind scattered fallen leaves across the path. Frank panted and felt the drumming pulse in his neck; and he recalled, as he often did, that his father died of a stroke at an age just three years older than Frank now. Nevertheless he hurried farther along, still anxious to be home. He was occupied with trying to enliven the flashlight when he tripped over something on the dirt path—it was all he could manage to regain his balance and keep from falling. . . . Somehow the wild motions corrected the flashlight and its blue beam unexpectedly illuminated Max's wolfish features as the big shepherd was sitting on his haunches at the edge of the yard, calmly facing the farmhouse.

Winded, Frank said, There you are, Maxy . . . holy crap . . . you nearly gave me . . . a coronary. . . .

Max appeared to pay no attention to his master. Even his long thick tail lay in a curled C on the ground, moved not even a twitch by Frank's arrival. Frank patted Max between his tall triangular ears, and the shepherd blinked once, perhaps in irritation. He was watching the house intently; in fact, given the angle of his head, the second story.

Frank turned and shined the light toward his bedroom window—and was startled to see a spectral figure at the pulled-back curtain, white night-gowned Mrs. Whittle, who must have been surprised too as she quickly stepped away as if caught at something unseemly.

Frank knew not what to make of any of it. He went indoors, locked the kitchen door behind him, pulled off his overalls and boots; then went to his room, where his wife had already returned to bed and her gentle snoring. In the morning neither spoke of the night's queer events, in the manner that one keeps a revealing dream to oneself.

▲

Fall had come in dead earnest to the village. Along Main Street the maples, elms and oaks burned crimson. Against the northern sides of the square's gazebo fallen leaves of yelloworange palette lay knee deep. Branches, becoming barer moment by moment, framed more and more of broken gray skies, sharding patterns like broken glass. It was the season of reaping, and prayers were raised to Saint Anthony of Lisbon, and appeals to a god of a fruit-

ful caprice. Through the broken skies flew birds of migra-
tion, from the soon-frozen north to warmer reaches far
beyond this homespun hamlet and its godly citizens, who
clung together in the harsh light and whose souls wept in
the dark. There was a chill at harvest time, and hoarfrost
killed the flowers of summer remaining. Upon the frost-
ed grass footsteps tracked of a night wanderer, bleached
away by a weakening sun. It was the season of reaping. Apples still tinged with forbiddenness tempted children and
adults alike, covered in sweet wonder warmed on stands in
the weakening sun. And darkness came to the edges soon
upon day's end, especially in Hollis Woods, where stories
filled the black spaces like goblins of your grandfather's
spinning, of your grandmother's weaving. It was the season of reaping. The woods sentineled along the edge of the
village like a disquieting stranger wandered there from a
place stranger still, and even autumn's fiery paint could not
amend their darkness, bleaching the beams of a weakening
sun and befogging bared limbs amassed against the black-
ening sky: It was the season of reaping.

▶

Harvest celebration was held in a field on Old Man
Stevenson's property, though Old Man Stevenson had not
attended the celebration for years. He would watch the
goings-on from his house, using Belgian field glasses of
tarnished brass he had brought home from the war, and
he would eat the fare brought to him by a delegation of
wives and daughters. The celebration was bountiful: tur-
keys, ducks and beeves, roasted slowly in firepits by dele-
gations of husbands and sons taking shifts throughout the
previous day and night. In the long, chill nights Old Man
Stevenson's homemade shine would be passed around, and
many a village youth had his first taste of hard liquor in

|·) |·) |·) |·)
Icy places hard reached inside,
Beneath defiled skin, beyond battered bone;
Anatomy of a smothered life becried.
        Into a hellish torpor each easily slide,
        To struggle against the violation done;
        Icy places hard reached inside.
Even inside oneself remains nowhere to hide,
As the swelling secret remains unknown;
Anatomy of a smothered life becried.
        For four, but three in which to confide,
        Each imprisoned in her loving home;
        Icy places hard reached inside.
All with innocent face piously lied,
Each imprisoned in her growing womb;
Anatomy of a smothered life becried.
        From ancient world this ancient rite,
        Performed to bolster the blackest throne:
Icy places hard reached inside—
Anatomy of a smothered life becried.

the small hours before harvest celebration. There were also potatoes, mashed and roasted and diced into salad. Corn, squash, pumpkins, beans . . . soups, chilies, all manner of gravies and sauces . . . canned preserves and jellies, bilberry, blackberry, blueberry, gooseberry, raspberry, strawberry . . . pickled eggs, pickled cucumbers, pickled asparagus . . . pies, cakes, tarts, puddings—but most plentiful were the apples: apple pies, apple cakes, apple donuts, apple pancakes, apples blintzes, apples crepes, apple streusels, apple bisques, apple muffins, apple breads, glazed apples, baked apples, fried apples, apple chips, apple taffy, apple ice cream . . . And there were the usual village legends: Mrs. Reynolds's rabbit stew, Mrs. Abernathy's quail in white gravy, Mrs. Johnston's minted lamb-chops, Mrs. Phillips's fried chicken and cornbread, Mrs. Whittle's chicken and dumplings, Mrs. Smythe's morel soufflé, Mrs. Moreland's honey-glazed pork roast. . . .

The traditional trio of Doc Higgins, Barney McCarty and 'Pete' Peterson provided the music with six-string guitar, viola and standup bass—the same songs year upon year, folk songs older than bluegrass, laced with harmonies of an earlier age.

Frank Whittle, who had shed his overalls for blue jeans that looked brand new and a plaid shirt, drank beer from a styrofoam cup and stood enjoying the trio's familiar tunes. The beer was a dark lager homebrewed by Jack Burnside. It was not especially cold but tasted good nevertheless. Doc Higgins picked his six-string and sang about wandering Willa, a young miss who went looking for her one true love, still not home from the war, a war unidentified in the song but more foreign than the one against the Kaiser and older than the one between the states. Doc's voice was a higher register than you might expect and a touch nasally, yet there was something soothing about its character that could become hypnotic, especially after a few ounces of beer—and Frank was already beginning to feel that drifting-away sensation.

The trio was in the bed of Doc's Ford truck, black with side panels of gray dust—Doc and Barney sitting on the bed's lowered gate, and Pete behind them with his standup bass. Near them a group had gathered dancing dances as old or older than the music itself. The dancers were all ages and expertise, but they reeled and waltzed and clapped hands and locked arms with the ease of many hours' practice, the elder exhibited more stylish flair while the younger were inclined to watch their steps and display a look of happy concentration.

Frank's pat line was that he danced like he had two left feet, and Mrs. Whittle would shake her head at Frank's audience and confidentially display three fingers.

Mrs. Whittle was among the dancers; ostensibly her partner was Mrs. Johnston but the complicated nature of the dance, with its continual switching of partners, made the idea of a partner all but moot. Frank drank the dark beer and watched his wife, who wore a floral dress of bright-orange poppies and moved with the litheness of a woman half her age. The fast-paced motions made her glasses slide down her nose and every now and then she would quickly reposition them—the only break in her otherwise faultless exhibition.

The resonating strings of Barney's viola overshadowed Doc's guitar-plucking and Pete's bass-thumping so that all Frank heard was the highcutting whine of the viola, even forcing Doc's voice to fade into the background . . . then dissolve altogether. In fact, Frank realized the noise of his fellow celebrants, who had been loudly partaking of the feast, had disappeared as well, so that all he heard was the piercing viola music, which now seemed to harken from an even earlier time, from when the very nature of music was defined differently and that definition had been long lost in the gathering epochs.

All the while he continued watching the dancers, and it took him a moment to comprehend that their movements had changed. Instead of woofing and wafting their way between one another, in a clockwise sort of weaving, they were now moving en masse in a circular motion, with each dancer articulating an independent motion of the body— uncoordinated yet somehow complementary, to Frank's way of seeing. Perhaps because of the oddity of the dance, or some trick of sun and cloud, but Frank could no longer identify his wife among the dancers, who had become merely gendered figures undulating as individuals, while, as a body, they counterclockwised to the ages-old sound of the viola's vibrating strings.

Some remote part of Frank's mind told him he was under a kind of spell or hypnosis but he was powerless to break free of it. The figures continued their primitive dance, both wild and precise, just as the viola captured patterns of notes that Frank had never experienced—only the mournful wail of a bagpipe even began to approach the sound. The dance continued . . . beyond the bounds of knowable time.

First one then another then another . . . broke from the body of dancers, and they were all adolescent girls. That remote part of Frank's mind told him it was a finite number yet he could not fix it: . . . seven . . . six . . . eight . . . They had become the center of the figures who now moved around them, encircling them. The teenage girls, whose bodies were illuminated as if by footlights while their faces remained masked in shadow, had begun moving in improper ways, wanton ways, and Frank thought he should turn away but he was transfixed and could do nothing except look at the girls as they danced like harlots in Old Man Stevenson's field, while the adults moved about them, complementing and thus encouraging their wicked gyrations. . . .

Sweat beaded into Frank's eyes, stinging them, as if he too were dancing wildly around and around the girls. His pulse pounded in time with the wincing viola. He and Mrs. Whittle had not been intimate for years but he knew the scent that rose up from the village girls, as potent as a warm summer breeze striking his face. He fought against his swelling desire, and he wished that he had ignored Mrs. Whittle's insistence that he wear his new bluejeans instead of his usual overalls.

He drank the remainder of his beer in one swallow hoping it would distract him from the whorish dancing— Frank had shut his eyes while taking the last drink and when he opened them the scene was returned to normal: A bright autumn day shined down upon his wife and the other dancers, whose movements were the familiar weaving and reeling upon the dry grass, while the trio contentedly played their antique tunes.

The song concluded, as did the dancers, and everyone applauded their efforts. Frank still felt the effects of what he concluded was a sort of waking dream. Mrs. Whittle came to him, kissed him on the cheek, and took his styrofoam cup to fetch him a refill.

As the dancers dispersed to get their refreshments, Frank saw Wendell Phillips standing on the opposite side of the dancing area. The two men fixed their gazes upon each other but immediately averted their eyes and turned shades of crimson, for each knew what the other had witnessed.

Pastor Phillips's hands were in his coat pockets keeping the coat closed, and he kept them there as he hurried after his wife and daughter, who had gone to the apple-pie table. The dancing had sharpened Mrs. Phillips's and Rebecca's appetites.

▼

The morning of the first snow Wendell stood on his front porch watching the brick walk disappear beneath the accumulating white. Perhaps winter could conceal the virgins' secret but spring would be another matter. A single snowflake clung for a moment to the eave above Wendell's head before breaking free and falling toward the steadily freezing earth.

The Curvatures of Hurt

The Curvatures of Hurt

It is a single soul dwelling in two bodies
—Aristotle

A

Winter had lingered into spring, and patches of heavy, wet snow were melting in the cold sunshine as Frankie walked with urgency toward Shirley Donaldson's. Water ran in the gutters beneath disappearing canopies of ice. It was mid-afternoon on a Saturday, the sort of day Frankie and Rebecca would have spent entirely together not long ago, one of them having slept at the other's house. She had not heard from Rebecca since they left school the day before, with Rebecca hurrying because she wanted to get a jump on her homework, she said.

More and more, Rebecca was at Shirley Donaldson's house. Rebecca and Shirley had been friends before Frankie moved to the village, but Frankie's impression was that Rebecca barely cared for Shirley's company. Frankie didn't care for her company. Yet when Frankie knocked on the Phillipses' door and Pastor Phillips, who always called her Miss Francine, said that his daughter was at Shirley's, Frankie was consumed by emotions that drove her to visit the Donaldsons too.

Frankie stood on their porch and knocked on the storm-door. No one came. She went back to the walk which led to the porch and turned around to look up at Shirley's bedroom window: She recalled the one time she'd been in Shirley's room, with Rebecca, and looking out the window in utter boredom and seeing the walk (then, with everything in the steamy green of summer foliage). Peering back, now, the bedroom curtain was drawn, and the window—the whole two-story house—was a sickly shade of pale. Frankie listened carefully, patient through spikes of chill wind, and perhaps there were voices to be heard . . . muffled and distant. She couldn't help seeking them, so she began treading through the yard's soft snow, around the side of the house, past the dormant forsythia bush, the voices becoming louder but only slightly so.

Frankie reached a point where the inarticulate voices were loudest. Frankie stood quietly, her mittened hands in her coat pockets, listening, and one of the voices was definitely Rebecca's. She couldn't say for certain that the other voice was Shirley's—something about it didn't seem right, its cadence, and its pitch perhaps, sounding almost like a boy's or a young man's even.

They were muffled through the basement window at Frankie's feet. Jealousy swelled in her. When she heard Rebecca's voice again, she squatted and knocked on the window. It wasn't covered, and incandescent light fell in a yellow patch upon the pane. The voices ceased. Frankie removed a mitten and rapped more sharply. A face appeared in the window, Rebecca's. It held so many emotions at once it seemed distorted, and Frankie barely recognized her best friend—*best friend*, that was how Frankie called her, but the phrase didn't seem adequate to their relationship, not to how it had been since the end of summer. Yet lately they had slipped back beyond that inadequate phrase to barely friends at all.

For a moment they stared back and forth through the small window, Rebecca looking up, in a supplicant's posture, her willful brown hair framing her narrow white face.

Let me in, said Frankie, motioning toward the front of the house with the bare hand holding its mitten.

Rebecca's face disappeared from the window, and Frankie went to the front porch to wait for her. Standing there, hands in her coat, she tried to sort through her emotions, which were myriad, sometimes complementary, sometimes conflicting—many inexpressible. She wanted to cling to the happiness she felt at seeing Rebecca, but anger, hurt and jealousy kept elbowing their way into her heart.

She waited on the porch several interminable minutes but no one came to let her in. She returned to the side of the house: the basement was perfectly silent, and even the patch of electric light had disappeared from the pane.

B

Rebecca Phillips waited anxiously in the corner. She knew that Frankie wouldn't give up easily. Her stubbornness was one of the first qualities she admired in her friend, but now it complicated things. Frankie must be upset. There was no help for it though. Shirley had reached out and shared something extraordinary with her because they had been friends for as long as either could recall, and Rebecca wasn't the sort to gossip . . . *and* Rebecca was Pastor Phillips's daughter, which meant something, to be connected to God in such a special way.

Overhead, the floorboards of the porch creaked as Frankie impatiently shifted her weight, waiting for her to appear at the door and invite her inside. For a long while she had stared up at her best friend through the dirty basement window, torn about what to do, wishing that Frankie hadn't tracked her down.

Frankie went to be let in the front door, and Shirley pulled the cord to extinguish the basement lights. Then Shirley spoke in the voice that was queerly edged: Rafael says we must wait here until she leaves us alone.

In a few minutes, Frankie returned to the spot by the window, and Rebecca watched her friend's boots and the legs of her black corduroy slacks—Rebecca safe from sight in the basement's obscurity. Finally Frankie left.

There, said Shirley. Rafael says Frankie mustn't know. We can only trust you—for now at least. What? . . . All right, yes, John disagrees . . . Yes, *Shout from the mountain top*. But, John, you are a minority of one.

Shirley was only a few feet away from Rebecca in the basement's gray light, and Rebecca searched the gloom for John and Rafael and the others—the number always varying because the angels came and went of their own accord, save for Rafael, who was Shirley's guardian and had been at her side these many months. The moment Rafael let his guard down, Anthony threatened to come, and Anthony meant her harm—not all angels were good and kind. In fact, they were as varied in their personalities as people. Sometimes, in poor lighting, Rebecca thought she saw dim, ill-defined figures around Shirley but only for the briefest of moments.

Shirley went to the table and chairs that were in the corner of the basement. Come on, she said to Rebecca, we must finish our game.

Do you think it's all right to turn on the lights?

Shirley listened for a moment . . . No, not just yet. Rafael will say when. What? . . . Yes, Marcus prefers the dark—his eyes can't get used to electric light.

They went to the card table that was pushed into a corner of the basement allowing space for only two to sit. A half deck of playing cards was stacked in the center of the table, surrounded by the remainder of the deck laid in a pattern of Rafael's choosing, by directing Shirley's hand. Meanwhile he would speak the meaning of the cards and their patterns in Shirley's ear—sometimes she would share his words with Rebecca, sometimes not, only nod and take another card from the deck.

They sat at the table, on metal folding chairs, and Shirley took a card. Light came through the small window directly above the table. Shirley shared the card over her shoulder with Rafael and whoever else may be watching. She listened to him, then allowed his words to guide her hand. She placed the nine of hearts at the end of the queen of clubs. Rafael explained its significance, and Shirley took another card, repeating the process with the three of spades, then the jack of spades. Finally she shared what Rafael had been telling her:

Henry lingers in his field, lonely, until he must look for comfort. He's creating all manner of mischief.

Rebecca wanted to ask what Rafael meant but knew to hold her tongue. Prodding only interrupted.

Miranda, Mary, Julie, Patricia, Sarah, Dorothy, Gloria . . . Frankie.

But that can't be.

Shirley tried to ignore the intrusion.

That can't be.

Shirley had taken a new card and was sharing it with Rafael.

What do you mean *making mischief*?

Irritated, Shirley looked at Rebecca. Maybe he'll tell us if we're patient. She looked toward the basement's gloom. Rafael, come back. She's sorry for butting in . . . aren't you sorry? Tell him, Rebecca.

Rebecca looked into the basement of shadows. Everything was so confusing. When Shirley confided in her that she spoke with angels, that they came to her at night especially but sought her at other times too, that one angel who called himself Rafael never left her—Rebecca wanted to believe. She had been surrounded by ideas of God and Jesus and the Virgin birth and the stories in the Bible her entire life, maybe surrounded by them more than anyone in the village since her father was the pastor, but for a long time she'd wondered . . . she didn't see signs of the Trinity anywhere, other than when adults said this or that was God's doing, something loving or something cruel, then some adult, oftentimes her father, would ascribe it to God's love or God's mercy or God's wisdom. But the reasoning always struck Rebecca as convenient, even when she was a little girl. She wanted to ask her father and sometimes did, but his answers were hardly answers at all, and he clearly didn't approve of her curiosity. Then she met Frankie, who was so smart and sure of herself. Frankie didn't seem to believe, not with her whole heart, but she was willing to fit in, and soon the church and its functions were opportunities for her and Rebecca to be together. On Saturday nights, Frankie began sleeping over, sharing Rebecca's small bed, so that they could ready themselves for church and walk there together, just the two of them. Rebecca's father and mother would've left the house an hour before to prepare for the service.

Then one day Shirley asked Rebecca to come home with her after school, just her—and when they were alone in Shirley's room, she told Rebecca about the angels and introduced her to Rafael and Marcus, and swore her to secrecy.

Rafael and Marcus were older angels, especially Rafael, who was from another place altogether and spoke with an accent. Marcus was from a past time to be sure, but not nearly so past and so foreign as Rafael—yet it was Marcus who was pained by so many modern things: electric light, the ringing of the telephone, the thump of the needle on her records when Shirley played her phonograph, the backfiring of Mr. Finch's delivery truck. That evening Shirley described the whole catalog of angels who'd been visiting her, including Anthony, the angel who'd tried to pull her hair and seemed to want to strangle her. Rafael protected her and sent Anthony away and said he would need to be watchful because Anthony would try to return.

Rebecca sat on Shirley's bed for a long time listening. At first she tried to ask questions but it was clear Shirley didn't want to answer questions—they hindered the flow of words she needed to speak. She'd obviously been keeping them dammed up for months, and now they were all pushing forth because Rebecca was there to listen. The angels told Shirley things about the village and about their neighbors, bits of gossip she'd never known but it was impossible to be sure if any of it was true. Shirley's story was fantastic, yet Rebecca wanted to believe. It would validate all the fantastic stories in the Bible, especially the ones about angels—Gabriel's visiting Mary, Michael's rescuing Daniel—and life would be better, simpler, if she believed with her whole heart as her father and mother did, as the entire village did.

Shirley must have sensed that her friend wasn't fully convinced. Rafael has told me something about *you*. Shirley's usually pale face was flushed, and her eyes were round and a little wild looking. The whole time she'd been speaking she held one of her bed pillows to her chest, gripping it fiercely.

About me? said Rebecca, from the foot of the bed, her legs folded beneath the spread of her wool skirt. What did he say?

Shirley hesitated. Perhaps I shouldn't tell you. She blinked and shifted the pillow in her hands. The pillowcase was crushed with the impression of her fingers.

Tell me.

She seemed to regain her momentum. Rafael says you've begun.

Begun, repeated Rebecca, knowing.

Yes, begun. Begun begun. You're a woman now.

It's not true . . .

Rebecca left Shirley's house that evening, sworn to secrecy, which almost wasn't necessary. She was so bewildered by Shirley's news that she would've had difficulty telling it to anyone, even to Frankie, who couldn't possibly accept the angels' existence. Rebecca was having trouble, too, even though she very much wanted to believe in them.

Г

Frankie didn't attend services the morning after she'd been left standing on Shirley's porch. She didn't try to see Rebecca at all that day. Pastor Phillips didn't mention Frankie's absence. He must've noticed that Rebecca and Frankie's friendship had seemed to cool these last few weeks. Rebecca imagined that he was most concerned about how the state of their friendship affected Frankie's faith. If he noticed his daughter's anxiousness, he probably would've attributed it to her rift with Frankie. For that matter, when she thought of it, her father had seemed distracted too.

At school, Mrs. Wilson was teaching them about Homer's *Odyssey*, and that Monday they were reading and discussing the hero's journey to the underworld. *His communion with shades*, Mrs. Wilson called it. Every so often Rebecca would glance across the room toward Frankie, both hoping and fearing to catch her eye, but Frankie appeared deeply interested in the ancient story and Mrs. Wilson's notes on the chalkboard. At noon, Frankie sat down with her lunch-bag next to Brenda Larson, who wore wrinkled plaid dresses and normally sat alone in the rec-room with a book open before her on the table. Rebecca and Shirley sat across from one another. Shirley left space on the end of her bench for Rafael, only as a courtesy Rebecca knew, because angels were not bodily figures, not exactly, and they had no need to sit.

Around other tables in the school's rec-room sat the girls who Rafael said were in trouble: Miranda, Mary, Julie, Patricia, Sarah, Dorothy and Gloria. Gloria was with her boyfriend, slow-talking and clumsy-footed Arthur Smith. If Gloria was in trouble, it seemed unlikely that Arthur was responsible. Yet Rafael's claims were too fantastic to be true, that Henry—or rather Henry's spirit, his ghost in other words—had visited the girls in their beds, in their unwaking hours even (Rafael often used odd phrases like that, *unwaking hours*), and lay with them and now each was with child. Henry Goodpath had been on a tractor, mowing the grass in Hewitts' field, when the old Minne-Moline turned over on a steep slope and Henry was killed. Mrs. Hewitt found him when he hadn't come in for lunch. That had been nearly two years ago.

Rebecca thought of the terror of becoming pregnant, the shame of it. Still, there was part of her that registered the hurt of being passed over by Henry's spirit, or rather it aggravated the old wound of being the girl that none of the boys noticed. Frankie's attention had done a lot to make up for that hurt. She looked over at Frankie, who was laughing at a joke she and one of her new lunch friends had shared. In her merriment, she quickly looked and found Rebecca's eye. Scalded, the girls turned away.

Δ

Frankie's dream: There is a long corridor, the floor reflective with wax. Along one side are windows, along the other, nothing—it is immaterial: a corridor with only one side. It is bright, the light intense. She walks along the bright hall with a vague sense that she is late to be somewhere, an appointment that carries with it an equally vague sense of dread. Something catches her attention, and she looks to the right. A pair of children are outdoors playing tetherball. One child is too small and the rubber ball on the rope orbits over her head, out of reach; it is pointless to try. She tries to see who the tall child and the small child are but their faces are turned away. She looks through the next window and the scene is changed: it is only an empty courtyard of grass and leafy bushes. She walks farther. She can smell the wax on the floor, tart like blood oranges. A voice calls to her, "Francine," the name her mother uses, used to . . . she recalls that she is gone, like geese in winter, but with a never-coming spring. The voice grows louder. She stops and peers out the window. Rebecca is standing close to it, her face nearly against the pane. She calls, "Francine!" Rebecca is in a white dress, like a baptismal gown, her leaf-brown hair curled in unkempt ringlets. Rebecca appears anxious. She knows that she should relieve her friend's anxiety and call back to her but remains mute. Rebecca calls again, "Francine!" Behind her, the children's voices cry out as if panicked. She leaves Rebecca at the window to check on the children playing tetherball. They and Rebecca should be in the same courtyard, yet they are not. She returns to the children's window and they are gone. The tethered ball bumps against its pole in the wind that has risen. A terrible storm of scab-colored clouds has sprung up and is approaching with malice. She realizes that Rebecca is in danger and tries to rush back to where she left her standing. The wax on the floor has softened and become sticky, clinging to her bare feet. It requires great effort to lift them. Meanwhile the storm approaches, nearer and nearer. Outside the wind sweeps across the bushes, which vibrate as if with current. Finally she reaches Rebecca's window, and her friend has moved away and is standing in the courtyard with her back to her. She may be watching the terrible storm or may be oblivious to it. She tries to open the window but it is shut tight, as if nailed in place. Her panic grows as she struggles with the immovable window. It may not be Rebecca at all in the courtyard, the wind slashing at the whipping white dress—it may be her mother, whose voice she cannot recall even in dreams. **Rebecca's dream**: She seems to hear the rhythmic squeal of the rusty chain for a long while before realizing it's the chain on the swingset grating against the bolts which secure it. She pulls hard with her arms to propel herself in a greater and greater arc. The old chain is cold and rough with rust in her hands, the wooden seat slick with age and use. The skirt of her dress, white like an innocent child's gown, billows with air at each forward thrust, then flattens with backward momentum. She is in an enormous green park with nothing but grass—no trees or bushes or flowers. In the far distance is a large building of brown brick, like a factory or a big-city high school. Where has everyone gone? It is an unimportant question. She is calm and content, except for the grating chain, which grows louder the higher she is able to swing. She strains to go higher even though she could fly off the age-slick seat. Her father is before her standing in the park wearing his minister's black with the white collar, clothes he saves for weddings and funerals. He is calmly watching her, a faint smile on his thin lips. They stay like that—she swinging and her father watching for a long while, contented. "Catch me, Daddy!" He raises his hands but he is farther away. At the conclusion of the next arc farther still. "Closer, Daddy!" His smile is just as benevolent but he continues to be more distant, and more distant, hands upraised as they are every Sunday toward Jesus on the cross, his back to the congregation. Panicked, she feels herself slipping from the seat. She mustn't wait any longer for her father to come to her. She releases herself into the still air. **Wendell Phillips's dream:** The congregants sit bovinely in the pews watching their pastor, truly with the blank expression of the cattle on Frank Whittle's farm. He adjusts his black-rimmed glasses, straightens the knot of his necktie, glances down at the Scripture before him, and reads aloud, "When he disembarked and saw the vast crowd, his heart was moved with pity for them, for they were like sheep without a shepherd . . ." He glances up at the congregation and is startled by a strange light emanating from the pews. He thinks for a second that he has neglected to turn on the sanctuary's overhead fixtures when he arrived and someone has finally realized and flipped the switch; but he immediately dismisses the idea. The sudden glow is coming from the congregants themselves. The pastor squints against the oncoming glare: specifically the light comes from an aura cast by each of the teenage girls— white light tinged in rose or ice blue or blushing lavender, framing their lovely heads. And the radiance queerly lights and shades the other members of the congregation, transforming their features into light and dark masks as intricate and mysterious as the moon's cratered and peaked shadows. The weird glow backlights the girls' faces, making it difficult to identify who is who. But neither the haloed girls nor the others seem to be aware of their nimbuses. The pastor has quit reading and is blinking against the harsh glare when just as suddenly the illumination ceases . . . and he realizes his congregants are staring at him quizzically. He issues a wan smile and recovers his place in Mark. **Shirley's dream:** Rafael smells like cloves, freshly chopped; Bertram an old dog damp from the rain; Charles an ear of corn freshly shucked; Damien the waxed floor near a boiler, hot in winter; Daniel chrysanthemum petals freshly picked and rubbed between the fingers; Edgar red brick still warm from the kiln; Edward sweat from a private recess of the body on the warmest of days; Frederic pine cones popping in an autumn fire; Garth chicory brewed in boiling water; Gerald a green apple cored before cutting; Henry cinnamon bathed in melting butter; John the pages of old books finally open after long-absent readers; Kristopher forsythia blossoms blown by a spring storm; Liam black earth spaded over, its insect world suddenly exposed to light; Marcus the musk of damp wool; Orlando the zest of blood oranges; Philip spring grass, newly mowed of a dewy morning; Samuel wild onions on the breeze in midsummer; Terrance the dust trapped in pine drawers; Theodore pumpkin pulp scooped in preparation of carving; Ulysses minced meat filling upon perforating the paraffin; Xanther, cucumber water, iced and in the shade; Zane the red wine of sacrament; Anthony English aftershave and the smoke of Pall Malls.

E

Frankie propped the bed pillows behind her back, pulled over the flowered spread so that it covered her legs, and took up the book on her side table, the library's copy of the *Odyssey*. It was a thick volume with green binding, old and often-read. She appreciated its smell and its feel as much as its words. Frankie felt exhausted, and she knew it was from the stress of losing Rebecca's friendship. Since her mother's death, when Frankie was eleven, she had not allowed herself to become close to anyone—to love anyone—because the pain of loss was too great and too thorough. It crept into all your corners, seeped through all the cracks, and wormed its way into the very marrow of your heart. It was only now at her loss that Frankie knew she loved Rebecca—the pain she felt proved it, like cornstarch sprinkled on an oily thumbprint reveals it and all of its contours, plain as day. She sat on her bed for a time and explored the contours of her loss, the curvatures of her hurt.

She opened the book to the part they had mainly studied in class: the hero's communion with the dead. They only had an excerpt in their school textbook, and Frankie wanted to read the entire section. The story touched her pain, inflaming it where it so long had lain hidden, giving her pain a concreteness, a shape and a substance, thus easing some of the terror of it, like a menace that has lingered in the shadows at last coming into the light.

Frankie gradually came to understand these things, in some recessed space of her mind, as she read about the Greek soldier's entrance into the murky underworld. The ghosts came upon him, thirsty for the blood of sacrifice he'd spilt in the gloom. Mrs. Wilson, their English teacher, said that the hero had survived ten years of horrific warfare, and one way of reading his account of his travels home is that of a man whose soundness of mind had been compromised—*by death in continual close quarters*, that's how Mrs. Wilson had put it. She didn't want to say Odysseus was mad, not so plainly, because Mrs. Wilson's brother had come back from Korea *not right* (everyone knew it but hardly anyone said), and he'd only been home for a while before moving away again. That was the story.

Frankie used the bed cover to blot the tears from her cheeks as she read of the Greek's encountering his mother in the underworld, in fact learning of her death that way. Odysseus wept too—each in sympathy with the other, for all their losses.

Z

Frankie woke in the night, wondered at the time, and tried to fall back asleep. She'd had strange dreams but couldn't recall their details, yet they'd left their strangeness upon her. She pulled back the covers and untangled her legs from her sleeping gown. Moonlight was etched on the curtain in her bedroom, which drew her to the window. She walked on tiptoe in an effort to avoid the chill of the wood floor.

There was a person standing on the walk before her house, and she recognized Rebecca's form immediately in the moon's indigo-tinted light. There appeared to be a second person with Rebecca, someone largely shielded by her friend's body and obscure in spite of the moonlight. Rebecca waved up at Frankie and motioned toward the side of the house. Frankie nodded and stepped back from the window, letting the curtain close. For a moment she considered leaving Rebecca standing at her door, as she had been left standing at Shirley's. She suspected it was Shirley who accompanied Rebecca, which made the opportunity for payback more than twice as tempting.

Frankie took her robe from the foot of the bed, and began to make her way downstairs. She paused for a moment at her father's half-open door and confirmed his quiet snoring. She walked through the dark living room and didn't switch on a lamp until she came to the kitchen. Rebecca hadn't knocked but she assumed she was standing outside the kitchen door, she and Shirley. Frankie used one finger to pull back the curtain over the door's window, and she saw a single dark figure in profile, who then turned toward the window and offered a little wave to her friend.

Frankie opened the door and Rebecca stepped inside.

Frankie peered about the night for Shirley, perhaps embarrassed to come forward, as she shut the door. She turned, What's going on?

Rebecca's blue wool coat was buttoned over her school dress, as if she hadn't been to bed. It wasn't as cold tonight as it had been but Rebecca seemed chilled. She wore gray wool socks pulled up to her knees, so that only her pale kneecaps showed beneath the hem of her dress.

It's good to see you, said Rebecca.

Frankie realized her friend was nearly at the point of tears. In fact, her eyes were red and raw as if she'd already been crying—perhaps finally sorry for the way she'd been treating her. If that's what was happening here—and Frankie ached for it to be—she wasn't quite ready to forgive her.

It's late, Frankie said, hugging herself as if she was chilled too when in fact she was oppressively warm with agitation.

Yes, I'm sorry . . . I wasn't sure I should come. . . .

But here you are. Frankie walked past her friend, pulled a kitchen chair out at an angle and sat.

Rebecca went to the table also and stood with her hands on the back of a chair. Frankie didn't invite her to sit down.

Why've you come? We have to be quiet, Daddy's asleep.

I have to tell you something (almost in a whisper), but I can't say everything.

You're not making sense. Frankie wanted to shout it. She felt her anger and hurt churning up from someplace deep within her, a place until that moment she didn't know existed. She swallowed hard to try to keep the emotions from erupting.

Rebecca fidgeted with a button on her coat. How have you been, how've you been feeling?

You came here at this hour to ask me that? You could ask me that at school—if you were talking to me. Frankie pulled her robe tight around her stomach and chest. She felt the tears coming but the last thing she wanted was to cry, to let Rebecca know how deeply she'd hurt her—though she obviously knew.

No, said Rebecca, it's not just that . . .

What then?

More fidgeting with the button, a new habit, Frankie decided. I, began Rebecca, have information . . . She began again: I know that you . . . More fidgeting.

For the love of God, spit it out! Frankie tried to check her voice at the last.

You're going to have a baby, blurted Rebecca, nearly pulling her button from her coat.

Frankie stared at her friend. What are you talking about?

You need to see Dr. Higgins, or someone—*there's a baby inside you.*

That's insane, that's impossible. You need to have The Talk again. Yet all at once the idea saturated Frankie's thoughts—and the things she'd been experiencing lately, the tiredness, the sadness, the sense that she was one step away—one insult, one rude look, one stubbed toe—from exploding, or from weeping and dissolving. Why do you say that? Frankie quickly stood and placed her hands on the back of her chair.

Rebecca tried to reach over and touch Frankie's hand but she suddenly put her hands in the pockets of her robe.

You'd better go. It's late.

I'm sorry to upset you, said Rebecca as she turned toward the door. Frankie neither moved nor spoke as Rebecca let herself out.

H

Rebecca had gotten as far as the street before the tears returned. A whisper of winter was still in the chill wind. Her tears turned cold as they ran down her cheeks. She felt a chaos of emotions whirling within her: shame, frustration, the anger bred of frustration, rejection, weakness. She took a hanky from the pocket of her coat, wiped her nose, and began walking toward home.

She told her father that she was spending the night at Shirley's—they'd be up late working on their history project—and she told Shirley that her father had chores for her at home, all of which contributed guilt to her tempest of emotions. She walked the quiet streets in no rush to get home. She wanted time to think, to try to sort out her thoughts, which seemed like fallen leaves caught in a sudden storm, swirling, flying every which way. She recalled how excited she was when she learned of the angels, and how excited Shirley was to tell her about them. Day by day Shirley told Rebecca more and more about the troupe of angels who surrounded her, the details becoming more and more precise.

But along with the excitement there was the anxiety and sadness of keeping secrets from Frankie, whom she wanted to tell about the angels but Shirley insisted they must be their secret. This was different though. Frankie was in trouble and deserved to know, sooner rather than later, perhaps soon enough to do something about it. Rebecca tried to ignore that her mind had jumped to that possibility, to forget that she could be a party to anything like that.

Why then had she gone to Frankie in the night? What had she hoped to accomplish, if not to set that possibility in motion?

These questions remained half-formed and unspoken in her heart, yet left the traces of unarticulated echoes.

She'd been walking slowly. She realized she was near the square, which was dominated by the gazebo, whitewashed in moonlight. She recalled the morning last summer that she and Frankie sat in the gazebo. It was an oppressively hot day, and a bee buzzed along the gazebo's rafters, as if trapped inside the open structure. Rebecca barely knew Frankie then, and on that morning she was irritated with her frankness, a quality they came to call her *Frankieness* when their friendship blossomed.

Rebecca stopped and looked directly at the gazebo, perhaps hoping to see the ghosts of their younger selves still haunting its shadowed interior. She was surprised to discern a dark figure standing among the shadows, watching her it seemed. He stood so still it was possible to think he wasn't there at all, just a trick of the light and the dark.

In fact the longer she watched, only a few seconds, the more she convinced herself there was no one there at all. She thought of calling out to him but preferred the idea that the gazebo was abandoned.

Rebecca put her hands in her pockets and continued walking toward home. She tried to put it all out of her mind—Shirley and the angels, Frankie's anger and hurt, and the trouble her friend was in, her father's moodiness of late and the strain it was causing her mother—and focus on something else. She thought of school, where she understood the problems put before her: finding the area of a triangle, solving for x, listing the major battles of the Civil War, knowing whose assassination started the Great War, identifying the anatomical features of an earthworm, recognizing trees by the shape of their leaves, conquering the chord shifts in *Moonlight Sonata*, baking a pie so that the apples stay firm but not hard, knowing the proper way to respond to a boy when he invites you to dance . . . if one ever would.

Then there was Mrs. Wilson's class, and the stories and poems they were assigned to read. There was some information she could commit to memory, which author wrote which piece, when the authors were born and when they died, but the stories and poems themselves were slippery. They had meaning but Mrs. Wilson wasn't inclined to tell them what it was. Instead they were supposed to grope around, inside the sentences and lines, the paragraphs and stanzas, stumbling toward meaning on their own.

She thought of the poem by Homer, about the Greek soldier and his wanderings from fantastic place to fantastic place—the island of the wind-god, the land of the cannibals, the coastline of the beautiful and dangerous women, and especially she thought of the underworld of the dead. He had to find the blind prophet who would advise him how to reach home. Mrs. Wilson suggested that because the Greek had been in that terrible war with the Trojans for all those years, ten years, that perhaps he wasn't visiting the dead, not really, that they were just a product of his imagination—*his wrecked imagination*, Mrs. Wilson called it.

Rebecca came to the corner of her street, Willow, turned and stopped. She thought that she'd been hearing footsteps which weren't quite in sync with her own, and there they were for a second before stopping too. She peered down the long brick walk of Main Street, its darkness broken here and there by even darker shadows.

The wind kicked up for a moment and it carried with it the smell of cigarettes mixed with, competing with, sweet-scented cologne. For a brief second Rebecca believed she saw the form of a man on the walk but it may have only been a trick of the overlapping shadows.

She hurried along Willow Street, nearly running, feeling both foolish and afraid. Convinced that the man was following her, she didn't dare look back. She reached her front gate and rushed faster still until she was inside her house. She shut the door harder (louder) than she might, and she bolted the door, which was never bolted. There were two diamond-shaped panes in the door but they were made to give only a blurred view of the world. She had to rise onto her toes to peer out one of them. Perhaps someone was at the gate, or it was only the shadows of limbs falling across the glass.

Rebecca?

She turned, startled. Yes, Daddy, it's me. The stairs were dark but she imagined he was at their top in his pajamas. I'm not feeling well, and I didn't want to get Shirley sick.

Be sure to gargle before you go to bed.

Yes, Daddy. She heard him return to bed, his parental duty performed. She took a last look through the blurring window and was surprised by a splash of light on the pane. She was confused by what she saw until she heard the growl of thunder: the first storm of spring.

Θ

Shirley tried drinking warm milk before bed but it did little good and she spent most nights awake. Having Rebecca over provided some comfort, though not much more sleep. The activities of the angels, their comings and goings, and their incessant talking, made it nearly impossible. It mattered not whether it was dark or light, Shirley saw them just as plainly. In the dark, the angels carried their own radiance, not a radiance that fell upon other things but it was like they were unaffected by darkness.

So as Shirley lay in bed, the lamp next to her switched off to make her parents think she was sleeping, she watched the angels and listened to their conversations, nearly all meaningless to her. **Rafael** stood by her bed, from time to time speaking to one of his fellows or commenting to Shirley. Rafael had dark hair and darker features. He wore a long shirt of crimson velvet tied at the waste with a golden sash. His black pants stopped at his knees and beneath were black stockings and black leather shoes with heels that added a few inches to his height. He often kept his fingers tucked into the sash with only his thumbs resting free. **Marcus** wore a gray wool coat with large buttons carved of bone, and trousers of darker and lighter gray stripes, gathered into tall black boots. His hair was as dark as Rafael's but his long, narrow face was much paler beneath a thin black beard. He tended to speak with his hands, and when they weren't gesturing excitedly, his arms were folded tightly across his chest—the position they would be brought to for dramatic emphasis after declaring his irritation at some modern mechanical noise. **Philip** walked with a limp and a hand on the hip of his bad leg nearly at all times, rendering himself in effect a double cripple. He wore a suit which had the cut of a military uniform, though there were no signet patches or epaulettes or sashes. His black hair and beard were neatly trimmed. Of all the angels he seemed particularly interested in the card game that Rafael directed Shirley's hand to play. **Terrance** was one of the strangest angels and at first frightened her but she'd grown accustomed to him. He was dressed in rags like a beggar and kept apart from the others. He was blind, and in fact his lids were sunken and shadowed, suggesting he had no eyes beneath them. His age-spotted hands remained clasped at his stomach. His unkempt hair and beard were gray-white. He continually spoke to himself in a quiet whisper. She once stood near him for a long while trying to hear what he was saying. She heard words but their patterns formed no meaning for her.

The activities of the angels were continuous. If Rebecca was there, Shirley would put her face against her friend's shoulder, and Rebecca would cradle her head, at least partly shutting out the angels, their movements and conversations, and she could sleep for a while. Without Rebecca she was especially restless, at one point even burying her head beneath her pillow. Shortly she gave up and sat with her back against the headboard.

Her father didn't have chores for her, Rafael said quietly.

Shirley turned to him, bearing his own light in the dark bedroom.

You know that already.

I don't know any such thing. She said her father wanted her home, and he wanted her home.

Rafael was silent but his look nagged her.

All right then. Where is she?

Rafael spoke to Marcus, nonsense about how the weather would be turning.

I'm sorry, Rafael. Where has Rebecca gone tonight?

He hesitated, defiant also. You know that too.

Shirley watched the luminous angels, whose numbers had suddenly doubled. Frankie . . . Rebecca had returned to Frankie. She always knew it would happen. Rebecca had turned away from her when Frankie and her father moved to the village, but she came back to her when she told her about the angels. She knew it was fleeting. Frankie had some hold on her—she had a hold on almost everyone in the village. She saw the way the boys and men watched her, even in church, after the children's blessing, even Rebecca's father. It was disgusting. Frankie pretended not to notice, but she ate it up, like thick-frosted birthday cake.

We should go there too. Tell her how it makes you feel, to be abandoned again.

It wasn't right, to go to Frankie's house at this hour to confront Rebecca. It wasn't right but the idea burned inside her, deep—perhaps in the place that is her soul. The angels became especially noisy and numerous, crowding her, making it difficult to breathe. She was sick to her stomach, and she felt a terrible pressure and ache behind her eyes.

Shirley threw off her bedcovers. She was still wearing

her robe over her pajamas. She weaved her way through the angels, most of whom paid her no attention. She had to stop to pick up her shoes near the blind angel dressed in rags. When she raised up he was *looking* directly at her with his sightless sunken lids. He'd ceased his meaningless muttering. His breath smelled of onions and a spice she had no name for. She never left the house, Terrance said … then turned away to continue his whisperings.

Shirley stopped in the kitchen long enough to put on her shoes. Then she slipped out of the kitchen door, careful not to let the screen-door bang shut. The night was cool and something on the breeze hinted of a coming storm, one that would wash away the remnants of winter. She went to the garage, which was her father's domain, and entered through the side door. It was a cramped space, taken up mainly with the family Ford Galaxie, but her father had a small worktable in one corner, and above it hung a safety-light on a black cord. Shirley felt her way in the familiar dark, one hand before her and the other on the cold metal of the car, until she reached the light and switched on the harsh bulb. She squinted against the painful glare.

Sometimes her father would get angry at her mother and at Shirley and her brother—over the smallest things, or nothing at all. He would get that look, something about the corners of his eyes, and his lips, straight across like he was pressing something between them, pressing hard. Then he'd go to the garage to be by himself, away from the family. Some weekends and evenings he spent nearly all his time there.

Shirley took down a Folgers coffee can from a shelf and removed the pack of Pall Malls her father kept there. The pack was open and half full. She took a cigarette and lit it with a match from the book also kept in the coffee can. She switched off the light and smoked in the dark, with only a thin beam from a streetlamp coming through a dirty pane of glass in the garage door. She snuck her first cigarette when she was twelve. When her nerves were buzzing, the rhythm of the long slow draws of smoke into her lungs was the only thing that would calm her. There were times that it was agonizing waiting for everyone to go to sleep so she could sneak out to the garage.

Rafael had of course come with her, and he stood watching the beam of streetlamp too.

After a while she was growing cold, so she took her father's old canvas coat from the peg where he kept it for working outside in cool weather. It was too big for her but its weight felt comforting on her shoulders, and the shearling collar smelled of her father's cologne, mixed pleasantly with a trace of the lamb's original musk.

She flicked ash on the floor of hard-packed earth and looked for a moment at the hand holding the cigarette between her fingers, the skin slightly sallow in the ray of streetlight. It didn't seem to be her hand at the end of the coat sleeve. The hand turned so that different fingers shone in light or in shadow, the smoke from the cigarette rising in the yellow light then sharply disappearing.

Shirley felt something running along her cheek like a fingertip. She looked at Rafael, who remained as still as stone, and she realized it was a tear that had trailed across her face. It gathered at the corner of her lips and she tasted its salt.

Other angels had joined Rafael and her in the garage, Marcus and Xanther and others. The space was too tight and Shirley felt again as if she couldn't breathe. She opened the door and hurried into the cool night air. For a moment she could catch her breath but she knew the angels would be upon her soon. More and more they came to her. She wanted Rafael to make them leave her be at school and church but he was quiet and raised no objections to them.

On the street, she tossed her cigarette into the gutter and began walking.

The dozen or so primary streets of the village were neatly arranged on a grid, like the paper they used at school to learn geometry, but once one went beyond the grid the streets transformed into roads and lanes, blacktops and highways; and then other rules governed their windings besides simple mathematics, conforming to boundaries of the landscape, the ownership of property, and the county's legislated needs. At the heart of the math was the village square, and at its heart the gazebo, ghostly white at the moment, lit by the moon, though increasing cloud cover meant to obscure the glowing disc.

Shirley was attracted to the gazebo's unearthly light, for it seemed like the light of the angels. As she walked Rafael was at her side, his radiance just at the edge of her vision. She climbed the steps of the gazebo, thinking that in summer the Passion would be performed there, the drama of the war between Heaven and Hell—and this year it would mean so much more to her. She imagined herself boldly coming forth from the audience, stepping past the adults who were playing the parts, ascending the gazebo's steps, turning—as she did now—and announcing the angels, testifying to their visitation to earth—to commune with *her*, unremarkable Shirley Donaldson.

And the angels would reveal their presence, one by one, to the wonderment of all who had gathered there, to the entire village. The rapture of it brought more tears to her eyes. The astonishment of everyone, especially her teachers and the girls at school who paid no attention to her, and her father. And they would ask her questions about the angels, when had they come to her, what was their purpose on earth. . . .

Rebecca would be there, silent, because she could have been part of the revelation, receiving everyone's awe nearly as much as Shirley—but Rebecca had abandoned her and the angels, denied them to return to Frankie.

Shirley's eyes burned with the hurt and the anger of denial. She rubbed them with the sleeve of her father's coat. As her vision cleared she saw a figure walking past the square. Rebecca, said Rafael at her side . . . or was it Rafael who spoke? His voice was altered, hoarser, reminding her of Anthony's, before Rafael had driven him away.

Rebecca, walking by, seemed to notice them in the gazebo, though they stayed as still as stone. Then she quickened her pace, maybe a little afraid, and Shirley was pleased. She and the angel waited a moment before leaving the gazebo and following her.

Shirley's feeling of betrayal was so poignant she wanted to lash out at Rebecca, to trip her, to pull her hair. She was coming from the direction of Frankie's house, and she was alone, which perhaps meant that Frankie had denied *her*. A taste of satisfaction tempered Shirley's hunger to do her friend harm. Still, they followed her, keeping their distance, keeping to the darkest shadows.

I

Frankie hadn't even gotten under the covers when she acknowledged to herself that it would be fruitless to go back to bed. She'd been waiting for Rebecca to come to her for so long—and when she finally did, it had all gone wrong. The anger and the hurt she felt came out only as anger . . . a petty, cruel anger. Perhaps the anger had been exorcised from her soul, somewhat, but the hurt was still there, burning painfully, and now she added shame at the way she'd treated Rebecca.

Her corduroy pants were folded over the chair in her

bedroom. She slipped them on, tucking her sleeping gown into them. Downstairs, she pulled on her coat and boots, then quietly opened the kitchen door.

Moonlight mixed with the breeze, which hinted at a coming storm. She turned in the direction of Rebecca's house. What if, instead, Rebecca had gone to the Donaldsons'? There was no purpose in considering the possibility. A better question was what was she doing at all?

The streets were quiet, deserted. It seemed the entire village was asleep except for Rebecca and her. Many were the nights Frankie lay in bed feeling that way: that she was the only wakeful person in the world. It was so comforting to hear Rebecca sleeping next to her in the twin bed, to feel her leg and hip and shoulder pressed against her own leg and hip and shoulder. Rebecca's sinking down next to her in bed, with the heat of her body rising and radiating through her, filled a space left vacant since the loss of her mother, which also marked the loss of her brother—the brother she never knew except as the bearer of her mother's death. She tried not to think of the baby in that way, to remind herself, rather, of his innocence, but the baby and death were forever intertwined, like that black-and-white Oriental symbol of the two fish wrapped around each other.

Frankie didn't comprehend how large the emptiness was that Rebecca had been filling until Rebecca was no longer filling it, and in fact her absence added its own emptiness to the terrible void. Frankie wanted to find Rebecca and somehow explain these feelings to her—why hadn't she tried when Rebecca was standing in her kitchen? Why had she been mute with anger, muzzled by a seething rage? Those feelings were gone now, leaving in their place only the exhaustion of having borne them.

The night breeze seemed suddenly colder, more wedded to storm. Frankie turned up her coat collar and began walking toward Rebecca's. She had only set off when lightning traced across the western sky, followed momentarily by a muttering of thunder. Perhaps it was a bad decision to be out but now she was set on the idea of seeing Rebecca. She was driven by a longing as if she hadn't been with her for many months, for years—and she thought of Odysseus, separated from his wife for twenty years, and her desire to be with Rebecca felt as keen and as prickled as the Greek soldier's.

Frankie's reverie was such that she'd been walking without thinking of her path, and she found herself near the square: another spasm of lightning flooded upon the white gazebo, then was gone. An icy drop of rain struck Frankie on the cheek, and another, and another. Instinctively she rushed to the gazebo for shelter. Inside, rain sounded like pebbles pelting its roof. The wind had risen and carried a cold spray to Frankie's face and hands. She thought that if she hadn't been so frigid to Rebecca, she may have stayed long enough to be caught at Frankie's by the rain—affording them the chance to make right their differences, and due to the lateness, they may have weathered the storm in Frankie's bed.

But instead here she was, cold and alone, perhaps with Rebecca driven back to Shirley's, to lay snug beneath *her* covers, holding hands and whispering above the rain.

Lightning revealed a figure in the square rushing toward the gazebo. In the glimpse he appeared to be a man, in a man's coat, head down. Frankie was startled and had no time to do anything beyond that reaction. The figure bounded up the gazebo's steps, probably only then realizing someone else was there.

The breeze flared and Frankie smelled cigarettes and shave cologne. The man was short, with long wet hair that clung to his face, and beneath the old jacket a wet skirt hung below his knees, like a gown in Doc Higgins's office—in all, making the impression he was an escaped mental patient (there was just such a hospital in Crawford).

The strange man seemed to be sizing up Frankie too, in these first few seconds of their encounter, standing facing one another. Lightning illuminated the square and their two profiles. As the flash fluttered the man rushed at Frankie, grabbing her hair with one hand and pushing her back with the other. Their legs tangled and they both slipped on the gazebo's wet floor, landing hard on their shoulders. Frankie had omitted a little animal cry of surprise and fear that was lost in the ripple of thunder.

The man clutched the collar of Frankie's coat with one hand but Frankie was able to jerk herself free and scramble backward until her back bumped into the gazebo's railing. Her attacker started to get up but immediately crumpled onto his side again, clutching the shoulder he'd landed on. He rolled onto his back moaning in pain.

Frankie thought it was her moment to escape but in a flash of lightning she realized that her attacker was even smaller than she'd thought, and before the ensuing thunder she heard him crying. Frankie crawled to him and pushed the wet hair from his face, a face she knew.

What are you doing, Shirley? Are you hurt?

But Shirley Donaldson didn't respond, in fact, didn't seem to know that Frankie was there at all.

Frankie looked out across the square and the rain had already let up. She looked down again: Stay here. I'll get help. You may have knocked your shoulder out of joint.

Rebecca's house was closest, and Pastor and Mrs. Phillips would know what to do—Frankie sensed that Shirley needed more than Doc Higgins's tending. Between sobs Shirley spoke to someone but not, it seemed, to Frankie.

Frankie stepped cautiously down the wet steps and hurried toward Rebecca's. When she reached the walk bordering the square, rain still falling, she looked back at the gazebo. For a half second it appeared there were several people in the gazebo but their dark and distorted shapes dissolved into a labyrinth of shadows with the next fissure of lightning.

Ted Morrissey is the author of four other works of fiction as well as two books of scholarship, and his stories and novel excerpts have been published in more than fifty journals. His novella *Weeping with an Ancient God* was listed as a Best Book of 2015 by *Chicago Book Review*. His essays and reviews have appeared in *North American Review* and elsewhere. A Ph.D. in English studies from Illinois State University, he teaches high school English as well as in the MFA in Writing program (online) at Lindenwood University. He has been a lecturer in English at University of Illinois and Benedictine University, Springfield campuses. He and his wife Melissa, an educator and children's author, have five adult children and two rescue dogs. They live near Springfield, Illinois. Ted is the founding publisher of Twelve Winters Press, modeling it after Leonard and Virginia Woolf's Hogarth Press.

CPSIA information can be obtained
at www.ICGtesting.com
Printed in the USA
BVHW031254041119
562856BV00001B/35/P

9 781979 274616